THE INHERITANCE AND OTHER DARK TALES

THE INHERITANCE AND OTHER DARK TALES

STEPHEN TALLEVI

CONTENTS

To my family.

EPIGRAPH

major ignotarum rerum est terror —
greater is the terror of something unknown

Titus Livius (59 BC - AD 17)

THE REACHERS

1935

It had started to rain, and the temperature was unseasonably cool for August. James stood on the lonely platform watching the train leave the station and slowly disappear around a heavily wooded bend. After briskly rubbing his hands together, he reached down for his traveling bag and started for the small station house. A weathered sign over the ticket window read "Welcome to Reachers, Sutherland County." There was no attendant, and the sparse waiting room was empty. James gave a weary sigh, took one last look about, then exited the station and began his walk northward along a single lane road.

It took thirty minutes to reach Birch Lane,

which wound its way down a little valley to Miss. Brown's cottage, where James had rented a room for the month. The unpretentious dwelling was tucked away next to a grove of pine trees, with a series of moss-stained stones forming a footpath to the porch, circling around a charming rose garden along the way. *Nice and secluded*, James thought to himself, *unlikely to be disturbed during my research.*

He made his way to the porch and, before knocking on the door, removed his jacket and hat, shaking as much water as he could off the garments. He smoothed his hair back then knocked twice.

A woman in her mid-thirties answered the door. She had an oval face with large, pale amber eyes whose expression displayed both a gentleness and a hint of sadness.

"Yes?" she inquired in a delicate voice.

"Hello, I'm James Carlton," he said with a smile.

The woman continued to look at him questioningly, so James added quickly "I called you last month. I'm the person who inquired about renting a room at your cottage for the month of August."

"Why of course!" exclaimed Miss. Brown. "How silly of me not to recognize the name. Please do come in Mr. Carlton."

Once inside the doorway, Miss. Brown eyed him for a moment before commenting in a concerned voice "Why Mr. Carlton, you're soaked through to the skin. Give me your hat and coat and I'll hang them up to dry. Wasn't Mr. Sanders at the station to offer you a ride? He's the only taxi service we have here at Reachers. He's also close to seventy-five years old, so his service has become less reliable as of late. Still, it's unusual for him not to be at the station for train arrivals. Please accept my apology on his behalf."

"No apology is necessary, I assure you Miss. Brown. And please, call me James."

"Very well, James it is. And you can call me Caroline, or Carrie for short, if you prefer."

"It's a pleasure to meet you, Caroline."

She smiled and took his hat and coat over to the opposite end of the room. A small fire was crackling in the stone fireplace. Two chairs were sitting near by. She turned their backs to face the fire and draped his jacket over the back of one and hung his hat on the ear of the other.

James took an instant liking to Caroline. She was of medium build with a fair complexion and rich, auburn hair. And those eyes. He had noticed them immediately, the peculiar shade of amber with a haunting, mesmerizing quality to them. He watched her as she arranged his wet clothes by the fire. She had an effortless way of doing things, accomplishing her task with quick but graceful movements.

"There, all done," she said, as she turned away from the fireplace, wiping her damp hands on her apron before removing it and tossing it onto the firewood basket as she made her way back to the doorway.

"Now, let me show you to your room."

"Thank you," James said as he reached for his travel bag. He was surprised to find that it was no longer by his side—Caroline had it in hand and was standing at the base of the stairs. "If you'll please follow me James, your room is just around the corner from the top landing, directly overhead from where we are standing now."

Two large windows made the room feel big and bright. A double pedestal mahogany desk was positioned in front of one, arm's length from a floor-to-ceiling bookshelf. A single bed, at the far end of the room, sat next to a full-length wardrobe. The mirrored door of the wardrobe reflected the image of James and Caroline standing by the doorway, her beautiful amber eyes were looking directly at him.

"I hope the room will do," Caroline said after a brief interval.

"Most definitely—bright, spacious and quiet."

"I'm glad. I'm going downstairs to brew a pot of tea—hopefully you will join me in 10 minutes for a cup?"

"Thank you. I'll be down shortly."

He unpacked his clothes and placed his journal and books on the desk. He turned to the bookshelf and quickly scanned the titles. One in particular caught his eye. A dark leather-bound octavo entitled "Pagan burial sites - an osteological examination (1742)." *Now this really is fortuitous,* James said to himself. He had come to Reachers to follow-up on Professor Johnson's work, who, some five years previously, published a paper on the peculiar bone structure of skeletal remains he discovered in the crypt of Reacher's abbey. Many displayed elongated forearms, and the bone itself had a unique composition, porous with numerous striations. The abbey was reputed to be a site of Pagan worship in the early 15th century by a sect who called themselves the *Reachers*, a name Professor Johnson believed reflected the unique morphology of their arms. The name was eventually adopted by the town itself. "I look forward to reading you tonight," James said out loud as he placed the book neatly on top of his own stack of books, then headed down for tea.

"So James," began Caroline after she had poured them both a cup of tea and offered him a warm scone which he readily accepted, "what are you researching that brings you to our far away town?"

"I'm an anthropologist," began James, "I'm most interested in understanding the origins of ancient Pagan societies and cults. I believe that the bones of those who practiced these religions may give clues why certain beliefs or rituals arose. As an example, Pagan shapeshifting practices appear throughout history. I would be interested in understanding how the belief in lycanthropy, the transformation of a person into a wolf, became associated with those whose index and ring fingers were of equal length. As a first step, I would look for skeletal remains that display this trait in regions where such rituals or beliefs where practiced. Now, as to my reason for being here, I know that the town of Reachers was named after a Pagan religion. Previous research suggests that the name may reflect some deformity in the arms of individuals, deformities that where integrated in their Pagan rituals and beliefs. I'm here to study their bones to see if I can connect the two."

After a moment's reflection Caroline said, "In that case you'll want to talk to Reverend Anderson—he's very familiar with the history of Reachers and can act as your guide when you examine the abbey crypt, which I presume you'll want to do? You'll find him working in his herb garden most mornings. His cottage is located a half-mile north of the abbey. It's no more than a half-hour walk from here."

"Thank you, I will seek him out first thing in the morning. I'm quite anxious to begin my research." He paused to drink the rest of his tea and then added: "Tell me Caroline, having grown up here, are you familiar with any of the folklore concerning the Reachers?"

"Oh, not much I'm afraid," she replied. "The Reachers believed that the soul resided in a person's eyes, and that they could forever maintain their youth by 'stealing' the eyes of younger, healthier people. My grandmother told me the occasional story, but I've forgotten them over the years. The one thing I do remember is a game we used to play. She would pretend to be a Reacher and chant 'Reach for the ground, reach for the sky, reach for their eyes!' At this point she would quickly reach out and pretend to grab my eyes and then slap her hands over her eyes. When she slowly slid her hands away, she would pull down on her lower eyelids which would cause only the whites of her eyes to show. A very creepy effect now that I think about it, but as a child I would scream with delight."

"Macabre to say the least," teased James.

She gave him a friendly smile then got up and started to collect the dishes before adding: "I usually prepare dinner at eight—does that suit you?"

"Perfectly, but not tonight I'm afraid. My apologies, but I'm dreadfully tired after that long train ride. I hope to be sound asleep by then so that I can have an early start tomorrow."

"Well then, I'll bid you a good night. See you in the morning for breakfast."

"I look forward to it," replied James pleasantly, as he got up and headed up the stairs.

Although his intention was to fall asleep early that evening, James made the unfortunate decision of looking through the book he had set aside earlier. Much of the content, not surprisingly, focused on religions associated with witches, which was of little interest to James. Much more relevant was the smaller section on Anglo-Saxon Paganism. It was here he came across a folded letter, wedged tightly between two of the pages. He carefully pried it loose, then set the book aside before unfolding the letter. It was, to his utter astonishment, a note by Professor Johnson dated July 1930, the year he published his last article. *He must have boarded in this very room five years ago,* thought James, *but why would he leave behind such an important book? And why would Caroline not have mentioned his stay here?* He made a mental note to ask her at breakfast. As for the letter, it read as follows:

Caroline told me about a game she played as a child with her grandmother, it involved a rhyme that ended with the phrase "reach for their eyes." I had already detected abnormal ossification in the forearms of the abbey skeletons (as I expected) but was now curious to check the orbital sockets. I spent several hours yesterday in the abbey crypt and made two discoveries—one of great interest, the other of grave concern.

First, some of the orbital sockets did show abnormal ossification. I'm unfamiliar with the unique bone growth and shallow grooves I observed, but have recorded them in detail and will present them to Dr. Buhl at Oxford for his interpretation when I return. As for the second finding, I'm not sure what to think of it, but I do not like it. After recording my findings,

I decided to wander deeper into the crypt. I came upon a low tunnel that appeared to be dug recently—it was certainly not part of the original crypt. I followed it for a short distance before I stumbled upon a pile of scattered bones. A cursory examination revealed the bones to be relatively recent in age—who would dispose of them in such a manner? Even more unsettling was that certain articles, such as a man's ring and a pince nez, lay nearby. I have decided not to mention my finding to Reverend Anderson. I have an overwhelming urge to leave Reachers as soon as possible. I will let Caroline know tonight that I leave by the first available train this week.

"Good God," muttered James as he finished reading the letter. He stood there in thought for several moments before folding and inserting it back between the pages where it was found. The book itself he placed in his travel bag—it would return to Oxford with him.

James had a restless sleep that night. He could not get Professor Johnson's letter off his mind. It was particularly disturbing in light of the fact that the professor never returned to Oxford, yet the letter suggested he was in a great rush to do so. As far as James was aware, no one knew what had became of the professor. He certainly had not published anything in the last five years, nor had his name appeared in any of the university directories James was familiar with. And what to make of the professor's findings concerning the orbital sockets? Certainly the eye symbol was deeply embedded in both Pagan and religious texts, but the notion of reaching "for their eyes" appeared unique. Combined with Caroline's recounting of her grandmother's portrayal of stealing someone's eyes, the picture that emerged was a gruesome one indeed.

At breakfast the next morning, James did not mention his poor night's sleep when Caroline asked if he had slept well. After some polite conversation, James decided to ask about the professor.

"Caroline, a thought occurred to me last night as I was dozing off to sleep. A Professor Johnson, an anthropologist like myself, published an article a few years ago about the research he did at your abbey. Did he happen to board here as well?"

"Why yes," replied Caroline after a slight hesitation, "now that you mention it I do remember the professor. I believe he was here five or six years ago. A very private man—took his meals in his room and spent most of his day at the abbey. Told me one evening that he had completed his research and that he was leaving the next morning."

"Did he say where he was going?" asked James.

"No, as I said, he was a very private individual. Why do you ask?"

"I was just hoping to send him my research to review once I was done here. I'm having a difficult time locating him at any of the universities." James shrugged his shoulders then added "Well, I'm sure I'll locate him eventually. In the meantime I best be on my way to find Reverend Anderson. I'll be back for afternoon tea."

"I'll have a batch of freshly baked biscuits ready. Good luck with your research."

James thanked her and made his way to the front door. Before stepping out, he turned back to look at her. She had her back to him and was folding away the tablecloth - once again he noticed her graceful movements, folding the cloth in one continuous, smooth motion of the arms. Efficient, beautiful to watch, and yet...somehow strange, almost unnatural in appearance. The harsh caw of a crow outside interrupted his thoughts, whereupon he turned and headed out the door.

Reverend Anderson proved to be most accommodating, providing James with a kerosene lantern and a couple of apples should he get hungry while examining the crypt. He would be back to get James around 2 p.m. The sky was already blackening and there would surely be a thunderstorm by late afternoon.

James examined several of the skeletal remains and confirmed Professor Johnson's observations. He was most anxious to move on and find the newer tunnel mentioned in the professor's letter. It proved to be deeper within the crypt than he had expected. James started down the tunnel and within a minute came to a circular clearing which marked the end of the passageway. He directed the light down towards the ground—bones were scattered throughout. He spent some time on hands and knees looking for the personal effects referenced in the letter, but found none. Feeling defeated, he got up and started his walk back through the tunnel. He had taken only a few steps when his foot kicked at something that briefly reflected the light from the lantern. Bending down for a closer look, he saw that it was a small piece of metal. He picked it up and brushed it against his shirt to remove the dirt from its surface. He recognized it immediately—it was a lapel pin from Oxford university. *God in heaven,* he thought, *this could only have belonged to the professor. Were his skeletal remains here? But that would imply...*

He could not finish his thought. A pang of terror suddenly overtook him. He spent several minutes to collect himself before making his way out of the abbey, where Reverend Anderson was waiting. James returned the lantern and exchanged a few pleasantries before heading back to the cottage, still trembling slightly, hoping the Reverend had not noticed. He decided he would leave the cottage in the morning and catch the first train out of town, no matter its destination. On his way back it started to rain, just as it had the day he arrived.

Caroline had an amused look on her face as she watched James enter the cottage. He was soaked through to the skin. "Well, you certainly seem to enjoy the rain," she said.

"Hardly," replied James, "it happens to like me. The feeling is not at all mutual."

Caroline gave a chuckle then said: "There's a clean towel in the wardrobe in your room with which you can dry yourself. I'll keep the biscuits warm in the oven until you come down."

"Caroline..." began James hesitantly, "I am sorry to say that I will need to cut my stay short. I've been an absolute fool and have left some essential photographic equipment at the university. I cannot accurately record my findings without it. It's my intent to catch a train back to London tomorrow morning."

"I see..." replied Caroline softly. "I am sorry to see you go. I have enjoyed the little time we have spent together. Perhaps you will return to finish your research sometime soon?"

"Yes, perhaps I will." James felt his cheeks redden slightly as the lie left his lips. "Well, I best go dry myself before I catch a chill."

James found the towel on the top shelf. He

wiped his face and towel-dried his hair before shutting the wardrobe door. In the reflection of its mirror he could see Caroline standing just inside the doorway. She was looking lovingly at him, a tender smile on her face. And then, quite suddenly, the smile died away. "I'm sorry James," she said in her gentle voice.

James frowned and turned to face her—it was the last action he would ever take. Caroline's arms, resembling long, undulating serpents, were beginning their age-old ritual. The ritual of reaching, *reaching for their eyes.*

THE KEEPER

1937

"I say Charles," began Albert, pausing to shift gears as the bright red Citroen began its ascent up a steep hill, "we should have reached Griffenhall a good half-hour ago. Are you sure you're reading the map correctly?"

Charles glanced over at Albert and gave a slight shrug of his shoulders. "I admit my navigation skills are limited Albert, but there is only one road from King's Lynne to Griffenhall and we're on it. But just to put your mind at ease, lets have James's opinion."

Charles passed the map back to James, who was sitting comfortably in the back seat, legs stretched out and chewing on the end of a cheroot he had not bothered to light since the start of their journey.

James pretended to study the map carefully for a minute (adding an occasional "Hmmm" for good effect) then handed it back to Charles. "I'm sorry to disappoint you Albert, but our navigator is correct—we are on the one and only road leading to Griffenhall. You'll definitely need to pick-up the pace if we stand any chance of getting there by supper."

This had the desired effect of making his two companions chuckle. Albert had been speeding for most of their journey, hitting 60 mph on several occasions, the automobile's "impressive cruising speed", a phrase Albert used, if not once, then at least a half-dozen times.

The three young men were on a short "sabbatical from Oxford" (as James put it), travelling around the countryside for a few days before the start of exams. Their car, the newly released 1937 Sports Citroen, was the most recent addition to Albert's father's collection, a prominent businessman who made his fortune in the booming chemical industry, producing fertilizer for the ever-growing number of farms in England.

"Quite decent of your father to lend us the new auto," remarked Charles, thinking of how painful the trip would have been in James' cramped and somewhat dilapidated Morris Minor, affectionately know as the "spinal compressor" among his friends.

"Yes, the old man has a kind heart, despite his reputation as a ruthless businessman," replied Albert. "In fact, he once—" Albert stopped suddenly in mid-sentence, adding instead "What's this? I thought father had the engine checked before lending us the auto!"

The reason for this sudden outburst soon became apparent to both Charles and James. Steam was escaping from the hood of the car. Fortunately, they had just come to the top of the hill, allowing Albert to switch off the engine and coast to a stop.

"What a spot of bad luck," remarked James. "And we were making such good time as well."

Albert gave a slight sigh as he shot an amused look back at James through the rear-view mirror. "I'm going to be a gentleman and ignore that comment James. Now come along you two, we'll need to move this vehicle off the road."

A clearing at the side of the road, next to a tall English oak, lay some twenty feet ahead, and the three men steered the vehicle to this spot without too much effort. Once there, both men stood aside as Albert released the latches at the base of the hood and yanked it open, all the while keeping his face turned away from the overheated engine. The two engine panels folded neatly together and came to rest in an upright position above the engine.

"How bad is it?" inquired Charles.

"Engine overheated, that's all," replied Albert. "We'll need to let it cool for a bit and top off the radiator with water as well. In the meantime, be a good sport and lend me your jacket, I need to wrap it around my hand so I can twist the radiator cap open. I promise it will be none the worse for wear because of it."

This proved not to be the case, however. Charles noticed a slight circular stain, the size of the radiator cap, on the right lapel of the jacket just as he was ready to slip it on again. He did not bring this to the attention of Albert, instead folding his jacket over his arm and commenting on how warm the afternoon was becoming.

"There's a house up on that hill to the right of us," James said, pointing. "Looks inhabited...though it could do with some repairs. May as well head up and see if the occupants will provide us with water for the radiator."

"I could do with a glass myself," added Albert.

The house, a narrow Edwardian construction unusually devoid of any ornate decorative features, had a gray, moss-stained door that was slightly ajar. Charles reached out and gave the copper door bell a few turns. No bell sounded, but a few moments later an elderly man appeared at the door. He was of small build, pale in complexion, and wore dark trousers and a Tweed jacket that would have been considered fashionable twenty years ago.

"Good afternoon," began Charles. "My apologies for the intrusion, but we ran into a spot of trouble with our vehicle. Is there someone in the household we can speak with that may be able to assist us?"

"I am the keeper of this place," replied the elderly man in a shallow but even voice.

"Wonderful," continued Charles. "My name is Charles Black, and these are my companions, Albert and James." Both men nodded their heads towards the elderly keeper, who ignored their gesture and continued to keep his eyes fixed on Charles. After murmuring a few words to himself, he said at last "How can I be of help?"

"Our car overheated. We were hoping you could provide us with a pitcher of water," replied Charles.

"I can accommodate that request. Please follow me into the kitchen. I will have to ask that your two companions wait here for you." The elderly keeper turned and motioned for Charles to follow. Both Albert and James feigned a hurt look at Charles. "Children," murmured Charles as he stepped into the house.

Charles had walked out a few minutes later carrying a white ceramic pitcher half filled with water, which Albert was now carefully pouring into the radiator. "Awfully queer chap, wasn't he?"

"I'd say," replied Charles. "Didn't say a word the entire time we were in the house. Didn't even acknowledge my repeated thanks for his help." Charles seemed to hesitate for a moment, then continued "Also, when he was at the door, staring at me, he murmured something to himself. The more I think about it, the more certain I am that he said *Ita vero, satis erit.*"

"*Ita vero, satis erit,*" repeated Albert slowly. "What does it mean?"

"It's Latin for *Yes, he will do.*"

Albert stop pouring the water into the radiator. He looked at Charles for a moment, then handed him the pitcher and secured the hood in place.

"I don't know about you Charles, but the faster I get away from this place, the better I'll feel. Just leave the pitcher at the base of the laneway where the old man can fetch it himself and let us be on our way."

They were just a few minutes into their journey when, quite unexpectedly, they found themselves driving up another steep hill.

"The terrain looked fairly flat when we drove off," said Albert in a perplexed voice. "Certainly I would have spotted a hill of this size."

The three men glanced at one another. An air of uneasiness had fallen over them. The car had just come over the crest of the hill when Albert slowed to a stop. He was looking to his left, where a narrow laneway wound its way up to an old house on a hill.

"It can't be," James said in a low voice.

After a brief moment of silence, Charles turned to Albert, ready to remark that, as unusual at it was, there could certainly be two similar houses in the area. But he stopped himself when he noticed that Albert's gaze had shifted, he was now looking at the base of the hill, next to the laneway. Charles leaned over to the right so he could peer over Albert's shoulder. There, just as he had left it only a short while ago, stood the white ceramic pitcher.

The men were leaning up against the car, lost in thought, occasionally glancing at the house, inwardly wishing it would not be there the next time they looked. The vehicle was parked under the shade of the English oak, one more uncomfortable reminder that they had indeed come back to their former location.

Albert broke the silence. He spoke rather to himself than to his companions.

"We can rule this out as being some queer configuration of the surrounding geography. There's no way we could return here in such a short time without having steered to the right for most of the trip. Alternatively, I would have to have made a few sharp right-hand turns at fairly short intervals. Neither happened. So...let us consider this further..." He left the remainder of his thought unspoken.

"Charles, I don't suppose you noticed if there was a telephone in that house?" inquired James.

"Telephone?" laughed Charles. "Do you see telephone wires anywhere in this godforsaken countryside?"

"No, of course not. You're quite right," replied James, turning his sights to the old house again. "It was a silly question."

Charles let out a long, slow breath before speaking once more to James. "My apologies for the curt response James, but I can't...I just can't shake the feeling that this event is linked to that house and the keeper who lives there." Here he paused, then shifted uneasily before adding: "I'd rather finish the journey to Griffenhall crawling on hands and knees than step foot into that house again."

An oppressive silence fell over the group. Charles had spoken that which had been on everyone's mind—that his entrance into the house set something terribly strange, perhaps even sinister, into motion.

Albert cleared his throat before addressing his companions in an even, calm voice. "I've been thinking this through and, if you and Charles are in agreement, I propose we do the following." He began to pace a little as he spoke. "First, you will position yourselves as lookouts at opposite ends of this hilltop. James, you will stand next to the road at the point where we drove up, and Charles, you will stand at this end, where we drove away earlier. Next, I'll get in the car and once again drive off—"

"Come now Albert, this is no time for levity," interrupted Charles.

"I assure you I'm quite serious—please, hear me out. As far as I can see, one of two outcomes will happen. If within five minutes of driving I do not see James at the top of a hill, then I know the road does indeed lead away from here. I will turn the car around, Charles will see me approaching, and before long the three of us will be on our way again." Here Albert paused. "On the other hand—"

"On the other hand," interrupted James gravely, "if you see me after a few minutes of driving, then we remain caught in this...this situation. So let me put forth a more sensible proposal—we forget about the blasted vehicle and start our way forward on foot."

But as he spoke these last words, he knew they sounded hollow. All three men instinctively understood that the house and its keeper would not allow this. They had been chosen to play out a certain fate, the outcome of which was still unknown. And so, without saying anther word, the three men parted, each heading towards their assigned task.

Charles glanced anxiously down at his pocket watch for the third time. Ten minutes had passed since Albert drove off down the hill. He turned to look at James at the other end of the road. Like Charles, he had just finished checking the time, and was returning the watch to his pocket when he noticed Charles looking his way. He nodded a silent "no" to indicate there was no sign of the car. Charles returned the same signal.

"What's taking Albert so long?"

James was now standing by Charles' side. Twenty minutes had passed since Albert left.

"I'm not sure he can come back, James."

"Not come back? What the devil do you mean by that?"

"The third outcome, James, the one Albert did not share with us. The possibility of him not returning. That's why he came up with the premise of keeping us here as lookouts. He did it to protect us, and for no other reason."

To protect us, James thought to himself, *Yes, that is exactly something Albert would do... protect us.* James took a minute to gather his thoughts before speaking. "I say Charles, Albert is like a brother to us, and we cannot abandon him, no matter what his original intentions were. Surely you must see that. We need to set-off and search for him immediately. Let's be sensible, he probably veered off into a ditch, perhaps injured or unconscious and unable to return."

Charles did not respond.

"Well, are you coming?"

Again, Charles said nothing. James turned to face Charles directly and was shocked at what he saw before him. Charles' green-blue eyes were staring blankly at the distant horizon. His pallor was ashen gray and he looked as if he had aged twenty years.

James stood motionless for a minute, then rested a hand gently on Charles shoulder and said earnestly "On second thought Charles, one of us should remain here. You continue to hold down the lookout post. I'll go and find Albert and bring him back. It won't take me more than an hour. I'll be back soon Charles, I promise."

Charles turned and faced James with his vacant stare. "I'll be here, waiting."

It was with a faint smile that James gave Charles a reassuring pat on the shoulder, then set off down the road.

A mist was slowly enveloping the country-side with the approach of nightfall. Charles had not moved from his post, not since James left over three hours ago. Darkness brought an uncharacteristic silence to the land. The feeling of isolation and loneliness took hold of Charles, and in a moment of utter despair, he turned in the direction of the house. He could barely make out its outline in the dark, but the door stood ajar, a faint glow emanating from within. As he watched, the door opened wider, revealing the keeper.

The sleek Lotus sports car swerved to avoid a large badger on the road, causing Robert to curse softly under his breath.

"That would have made a sizable dent Robert," remarked William. "Wouldn't do to show up at a new client with roadkill all over the fender and hood."

"You got that right. Damn beast almost attacked us."

"Must have been hungry," commented William. "Speaking of which, we left King's Lynne a couple of hours ago. I would have grabbed a bite to eat had I known the drive to Griffenhall was this long."

"Agreed. The road map made the distance seem no more than an hour."

"Outdated map I guess," remarked William.

Robert reached for the map on the dashboard and read the cover. "Esso 1967 road map for South and West England. Couldn't get more current than that." He tossed the map back onto the dashboard.

William stifled a yawn and rested his elbow out of the open car window. A few seconds later he pointed to the right and added "Careful, another large badger by the shoulder up ahead," then continued sarcastically, "Given the steepness of this hill the damn thing is going to die of a heart attack before any car gets a chance to kill it."

They were just approaching the crest of the hill when the car stalled, then came to a complete stop. Both men stared at each other in disbelief. Robert tried the ignition several times—the engine was dead.

"This can't be happening," lamented William, "we're already an hour late for our meeting."

Once out of the car, both men headed for the shade provided by an old English oak by the side of the road. It was William who spotted the house first.

"Looks abandoned, but I image most of the isolated homes around here do. Let's check it out. If there's no phone they may at least have some sort of vehicle for us to borrow."

"With the luck we're having today they're probably bicycles – with both tyres flat. Alright, lets get going and hope for the best."

It was William who tried to ring the copper doorbell. No bell sounded, but shortly after the door opened and an elderly man appeared. William detected a great sadness behind the piercing green-blue eyes that greeted him. And his clothes, although outdated, were of good quality, except for the faint circular stain on one of the lapels.

"We've had some car trouble," began William, "we were hoping...."

The old man continued to stare at William as he spoke, his green-blue eyes brightening as he whispered ever so softly *"Ita vero, satis erit..."*

THE INHERITANCE

1831

Richard Hartley, twenty-seven years of age, good-looking with light blue eyes and wavy brown hair, stood just inside the entrance gate, the shade of a large elm providing some relief from the heat of the midday sun. He was admiring the imposing facade of Elliot House, a stately manor surrounded by ten acres of land and bordered by dense woodland to the north and east. The estate was built upon a prominent hill at the outskirts of Easby village, and until recently, belonged to Sir Elliot, Richard's great uncle. Sir Elliot fell victim to a persistent cough after returning from a short excursion foxhunting in the vicinity of Barnard Castle and passed away of consumption several weeks later. As a childless widower, Sir Elliot had named Richard, his only surviving relative, as heir and executor of his estate.

Sir Elliot's solicitors, Henwood & Thomson, had communicated with Richard a fortnight ago, informing him of his uncle's demise and that Richard was the sole beneficiary of his last will and testament. Upon the news, Richard sold his few possessions, gave notice to his employer (he worked as a clerk at Sheffield and Hallamshire Bank) and hired a private chaise to transport him to Elliot House, as he could now afford such luxury. The distance was less than eighty miles, but the journey proved unexpectedly long. A severe thunderstorm hampered the journey early on, and an outbreak of equine influenza earlier that summer meant that the coaching inns had no horses to let for the subsequent stages of Richard's journey. The entire trip had to be completed by the original pair of horses, necessitating frequent and prolonged stops so that the animals could feed and rest. Richard had planned to arrive at Elliot House on Saturday morning, but it was not until noon of the following day that the chaise drew up to the front gate, leaving Richard at the spot where he now stood.

Reaching for the suitcase by his side, he proceeded, somewhat hesitantly, along the wide gravel path leading to the front entrance.

Steady on, he thought to himself. *This is all yours now, no need to be shy.*

He picked-up his pace, soon reaching the front steps which he took two at a time, managing not to knock the bottom of his heavy suitcase as he did so. He paused at the front entrance to catch his breath, then removed the latch key provided by Henwood & Thomson from the bill compartment of his wallet. He tapped the key a few times on his palm while studying the door—a solid oak, six-panel affair bordered on each side by white columns, across the top of which ran a classically engraved frieze.

"Well Richard," he said pensively to himself, "a new life awaits you beyond this door. A life of leisure and, let us hope, much happiness. I guess it would be appropriate to say a few words of thanks to Sir Elliot before entering." He was silent for a moment, then said:

"Thank you kindly uncle…I will be forever grateful…"

Not knowing what more to say, he looked down at his feet while stroking his chin for a minute, then lifted his head and with a slight shrug of his shoulders added:

"Forgive me uncle, I'm not very good with speeches, but know that I am truly thankful…" Pausing to reflect once more on his own life, Richard went on, "I presume the servants will address me as 'Master Richard'—I can hear my manservant now, greeting me with 'I understand Master Richard was a most accomplished bank clerk in Sheffield…'" He chuckled at this before continuing, "Doesn't quite compare to uncle's adventurous life, making his fortune in India as an exporter of raw goods. Well, not something I have to concern myself with today, as there are no servants about—I'm sure they are happy enough to have the weekend off. I'm certainly glad they are not here—it grants me the time to explore the house on my own." At this point he gently shook his head disapprovingly and said, "But come now Richard, this will never do—enough of this idle chatter, it's time to enter your house."

The entrance hall was elegantly but sparsely decorated, as were many of the other rooms in the house. The second floor had six bedrooms, including a very large master suite which Richard believed to be the size of his previous flat (no doubt an exaggeration on Richard's part). On the ground floor was the kitchen, sitting room, conservatory, dinning and drawing rooms, as well as the study.

Now this is interesting, thought Richard as he stepped into the study. The character of the room was in keeping with the general decor of the house—Wedgwood blue walls with a few large portraits in gilded frames. A mahogany, leather-top desk faced two large windows, and waist-high barrister bookcases lined one wall. It was the incongruous item standing alone on the opposite wall that had caught Richard's attention—a large vitrine cabinet. The display unit rested on square tapered legs that ended in brass cloven feet. The woodwork was accented with a finely carved, ophidian design, and two glass doors enclosed four shelves against a mirrored back. The shelves themselves were filled with an odd assortment of strange and exotic objects.

"Why, this is a curio cabinet," said Richard excitedly. "I had no idea uncle was such an avid collector."

Swinging the doors open, Richard proceeded to examine the items, each of which was identified by a neatly scripted museum label, each describing the object. A shrunken head on the bottom shelf was the first item to catch his attention.

"Ghastly object," he said, removing it from the shelf gingerly. He reached for its label and read, "Head of Captain Antonio de Herrera, Shipwrecked, Ecuador Expedition, 1699."

So, such things really do exist, he thought, *I was skeptical when Charles told me about them years ago —he was always telling tall tales to his classmates. If I remember his gruesome account correctly, the flesh is peeled back from the skull, then the bones and brain are removed and replaced with sand as the skin is stitched back together. What a frightful way to end one's life. May his soul rest in peace.* He carefully returned the head to its spot. Next to it was a pair of Hindu fakir's sandals. They were studded with dozens of rusty iron spikes that projected up through the soles. Richard tapped the spikes cautiously with his forefinger. *They really are quite sharp—amazing how these fakirs were able to conquer physical pain.*

Other items Richard examined included a preserved specimen in a jar that looked like a monstrous worm, at least three feet in length, an Egyptian mummified cat, and a clockwork automaton of a singing bird in a lovely gilded cage, its tune and head movements extremely lifelike. He had just started to shut the cabinet doors when he spotted a section of a skull on the far corner of the top shelf.

What do we have here? The bone was from the front of a skull, the portion surrounding the ocular sockets and nasal cavity. *Resembles a mask one would wear to a masquerade ball—far more gruesome, of course. Let's see what the label tells us.* The label was in a different penmanship than the others, and simply read: 'See through the eyes of a witch.'

Richard gave a short laugh upon reading this

and exclaimed, "Oh come now uncle, this really is going too far!"

He took the bone mask off the shelf, turned towards the window and held it at arm's length, aligned with his sightline. The view through the eye sockets was blurred, he could not make out either the desk or windows that were but twenty feet in front. His first reaction was to thrust his finger through the eye holes to see if there was a lens present—there was not.

Queer, thought Richard, *must be a trick of the light.*

He repeated his action, but this time he brought the bone slowly towards his face.

How curious, the room is coming slowly into focus, as if I were adjusting the eyepiece on a spyglass...

Richard continued this movement until the skull came in contact with his own face.

Unbelievable, everything is so crisp and clear, superior to my own eyesight.

He was still holding the skull piece to his face when he felt a slight pressure against his forehead. His hands moved instinctively to remove the bone mask, but they came away empty. The mask remained attached to his face. There was a tightening in his throat as panic slowly overtook him—the pressure of the bone against his face was beginning to increase. He turned towards the cabinet and saw his reflection in the mirror. The bone mask was being absorbed into his face. He could feel and hear his own flesh sucking the bone in, folding over it as it sunk deeper into his flesh, driving the bone ever closer to his own skull. He let out an agonizing scream, falling to his knees as he clutched at his face. His head spun violently, and a moment later he collapsed.

Richard awoke with a start to the call of a blackbird singing by the open window. It took a few moments for the fog in his brain to dispel, at which point he groaned and rose to his feet unsteadily. Bright sunlight streamed through the study windows, a sign that he had not been unconscious for long. Slowly, and with a feeling of dread creeping upon him, Richard faced the cabinet and looked at his reflection in the mirror. His face bore no sign of the bone mask. He ran his hands over his face, opened his mouth wide, raised his eyebrows, and puffed-out his cheeks, all to reassure himself that the mirror was indeed reflecting his true image. Satisfied, he took a step back and glanced upward at the spot where the bone mask originally lay—it stood empty.

Staring pensively at the shelf, his addled mind struggled to make sense of what occurred in the room. Did he hallucinate such terror while having a seizure or paroxysm of fear? He had certainly never experienced either before, but handling such hideous objects may have triggered the unexpected and violent response.

Turning away from the vitrine, he began to look about the study for the bone mask. It was during this search that a terrible realization hit him—everything in the room looked sharper, more defined, as if he were looking through...

"God in heaven, no..." he cried under his breath.

He placed the tips of his fingers on his forehead, and this time pressed hard as he felt around his temple. His fingers stopped an inch above his eyebrows. Yes, he could feel a slight ridge. Carefully he ran his fingertips along it—

the path they outlined was that of the bone mask.

*This cannot be—it's too fantastic, and yet...*Here again he ran his fingers along his forehead. There was no mistaking what lay beneath his skin.

"Damn you uncle!" he suddenly cursed out loud, his voice a mixture of outrage and fear.

Looking frantically about, he spotted a bronze candlestick resting on the desk. Seizing it, he marched over to the curio cabinet, raised it over his head as if ready to strike, only to hesitate before slowly lowering his arm to his side, letting the candlestick fall to the ground. He let out a long sigh, telling himself:

Get a hold of yourself Richard. Destroying the cabinet will resolve nothing...there may exist an object that can aide you, as remote as that possibility might seem to you now...

Feeling defeated and still in a state of disbelief, he made his way to the window, opened it fully, and leaned his head out, taking in a few deep breaths of the warm summer air. He remained there for several minutes, looking out at the vast and well-kept grounds. To the east, he spotted a paddock with a small stable near by. He thought:

A long ride is exactly what I need to help clear my head and think things through. I'm sure there must be a stablehand about to feed and turnout the horses.

No sooner had he finished this thought than a lad emerged from the stable leading a muscular, bay-coloured horse to the paddock.

Richard was glad to escape into the open air, cantering down a narrow lane that wound its way through the rolling countryside. He soon caught sight of some ruins upon a distant hill. *It looks like the ruins of a castle,* Richard said to himself, *can't be more than three or four miles away. As good a spot as any to rest the horse and think of what I should do next.* Having made up his mind, he gently twitched the reins towards the castle, the horse changing directions as it moved forward.

He arrived an hour later, approaching by way of the gate entrance. There was very little of the castle standing, the crumbled outer walls reaching a height of not more than twenty feet. Opposite the rear wall stood a copse of tall ash trees, their dense canopies casting a welcoming carpet of shade below. The horse followed the gravel path that ran along the outer wall, turning inward towards the trees once it cleared the remains of the rear tower. It was now that Richard received the second great shock of his life. There, on the gnarled branch of a nearby tree, was a woman hanging by the neck, her body gently swinging to and fro. Sections of the tree trunk were also aflame, lending a surreal atmosphere to the scene, like a depiction of hell from one of Giotto's paintings. As Richard stared in disbelief, the woman's body gave a series of spasmodic twitches. *Good Lord,* his brain screamed, *the woman is still alive!* Galloping full speed towards the gallows tree, he reached out to grab the woman as he rode up next to her, his other hand pulling hard on the reins to stop the horse. But his action proved futile, as his hand grasped at nothing but emptiness. There was no woman...no sign of a hanging...no burning tree.

With trembling hands, Richard dismounted his horse, his weak knees almost giving way as his feet hit the ground. He made his way unsteadily to the tree and leaned his back against its trunk before sliding slowly down to a sitting position, burying his head in his hands.

I have gone insane...utterly insane, he murmured to himself.

He sat there for several minutes, a look of incredulity on his ashen face. After a quarter of an hour, he had overcome enough of his shock to consider his situation further. *There is only one thing to do,* he told himself, *I must head back to London and seek treatment for these wild hallucinations. As for...,* he could not get himself to say the object's name, but instead rubbed his hand along his forehead, *...perhaps that is just a delusional disorder. Didn't mother tell me that Aunt Mary believed she had a second set of teeth in her throat and would eat only liquid foods for fear of choking. It may be that insanity runs in our family. Yes...I see now that I must leave for London, it is my only hope.*

He rose and brushed the leaves and grass from his trousers, after which he noticed a dark residue on his fingers, like the soot left on one's hands from handling a fireplace poker. With furrowed brows he inspected his hands, then turned to examine the trunk of the tree, slowly making his way around it, occasionally stopping to run his fingers along a crack or wound in the bark.

So, the tree was set ablaze recently. There are numerous spots where the bark is scorched and discoloured by fire damage. And if my vision of the tree is true... he turned his head towards the gnarled branch before finishing his thought, *...then the lynching of that poor woman may be true as well...*

The thought disquieted him greatly. So much so, that a dreadful conviction was beginning to take hold of his mind, a belief that his uncle was somehow connected to this horrid event. *No, more than connected,* he thought, *uncle was somehow responsible for what happened here.*

The wind had suddenly died down, and a sepulchral silence slowly engulfed the castle grounds. Richard walked over to his horse who had become restless.

"Yes, I find the silence deafening as well," he told the animal, patting its neck as he took hold of the bridle to lead it back towards the open countryside. "Let's leave this foul place and return home. I am going to delay my trip to London until I discover what took place here.

I believe the best place to start is to question Frederick when he returns tomorrow. He's been—I should say was—Sir Elliot's manservant for over twenty-five years. I can't imagine he would be ignorant of this affair. The question is..." he stopped and addressed his horse at this point, "...will he tell me?" He gave the horse another comforting pat on the neck before continuing. "The lawyers told me he was extremely loyal to uncle, so he may not be too forthcoming with what he knows. Still, he is accountable to me now, and I shall do my best to get the story from him."

Mounting his horse, Richard rode slowly back to Elliot House.

Richard slept soundly that night, awakening well after daybreak. Following his bath and a light breakfast, he was introduced to the house staff, receiving a brief but cordial welcome. Richard himself thanked the servants for their years of service to his uncle, and said he looked forward to their continued loyalty.

"Does master Richard require anything

further this morning?" inquired Frederick once the servants had left.

"I do have a few questions regarding uncle's affairs that you may be able to answer, or at least direct me to those who can. Let us meet in the study in ten minutes."

"Certainly, sir."

Richard was sitting at the desk when Frederick arrived. He motioned for him to have a seat across from him.

"I'd prefer to stand, if you don't mind, sir."

"By all means Frederick." Richard leaned slightly forward before continuing, resting his elbows on the desk. "I wanted to ask you about a servant that may have worked here recently, I'll explain why in a moment." Here Richard paused in order to recollect what he could of the hanged woman. "I have little information, but she was about five feet tall, red wavy hair and fair-skinned. Owned a pair of black leather-tip shoes, which I assume is not a common item among servants, given their premium cost."

"I believe there was someone who worked here with that description, sir, but she is no longer employed here."

"When did she leave?"

"Autumn of the previous year, if I remember correctly, sir."

"And why did she leave?"

"Well sir," Frederick began, somewhat hesitantly, "she did not get on well with the other servants and so...was asked to leave."

Richard leaned back in his chair and shook his head slowly. *He's being evasive. I'll need to take a more direct approach if I hope to get the truth from him.*

"I'm sorry Frederick, but I do not believe you. I know you were very loyal to Sir Elliot, but you are accountable to me now. Shall I tell you what I know to be true? The poor woman was hanged to death by the castle ruins, and Uncle Elliot was somehow involved, if not responsible, for this sinister affair."

The statement had the desired effect. A pallor overspread Frederick's face, and his entire body shook. Richard sprang from his seat and rushed to Frederick's side, seizing his arm to steady him before leading him to a nearby chair.

"Have a seat and try to calm your breathing.

I'll go fetch a glass of water. Don't try to get up, I shan't be a minute."

Richard returned soon after and handed a glass to Frederick, who had, to some small degree, composed himself. He took one or two sips before addressing Richard in a shallow voice:

"Thank you for the water master Richard. Please forgive my reaction, it was most inexcusable."

"Not at all," replied Richard, as he seated himself across from Frederick. "But you must now tell me all that you know of this matter. I take it from your response that the story is a most unpleasant one."

"It is indeed, sir. I do not know how you came to know about this dreadful episode, but it will come as a great relief to finally tell someone all that I know...or suspect."

Frederick took another sip of water before continuing, his hand visibly trembling.

"Three years ago, your uncle decided to sell his export business. He was getting on in years, and the annual voyages to India were beginning to take a toll on his health. When Sir Elliot took his final journey home that spring, he did not come alone. He was accompanied by a ten-year-old girl, the daughter of a good friend of his, Lieutenant Barrett. One week before Sir Elliot's departure from India, the lieutenant and his wife were in a terrible accident, their carriage toppling over a steep embankment during an outing to a friend's country home. His wife died at the scene; the lieutenant died in hospital two days later. Before he passed away, he gave custody of his daughter to your uncle, who promised he would take the child back to England with him. This he did, but as a childless widower, your uncle placed the girl under the care of Lydia, the housekeeper. She is the woman you are inquiring about."

Frederick paused to turn his gaze towards the open window before continuing, his voice steadier now.

"Lydia and the girl, Eleanor was her name—a lovely child, so kind and caring for her age—lived together in the servants' quarters. The two of them grew very close, Lydia caring for her as if she were her own child. At age eleven, your uncle formally employed Eleanor as a servant.

She was assigned light duties, helping to tidy and dust the rooms on the first floor.

"One evening, after having prepared Sir Elliot's room for bed, I came downstairs to see if the master required anything further before I retired for the night. It was his custom to spend much of his evening in his study reading. To my surprise, I heard master Elliot speaking to a woman as I approached the study, the door having been left slightly ajar. I found this most unusual, as he had few visitors in the evening. I was about to turn away when I heard the woman say in a sharp voice, 'You thief! How could you profit so from a child? I will not allow you to get away with this...' There was no mistaking the voice—it was that of Lydia.

"I know I should have turned and walked away, as the conversation was no business of mine. But I did not. I remained just outside the door, listening.

"'You witch! How could you know?' came the master's reply to Lydia's accusation. I could sense an undertone of fear in his voice as he said this. There followed a muffled scream, and then silence. I was sure the master had struck her. I could not believe him capable of such brutality, but I told myself it was not my place to intervene. I simply walked quietly away, and have regretted my act of cowardice ever since..."

There was a deep sadness in his voice as he spoke these last words. He continued to stare out the window, lost in thought. His eyes became watery as he held back tears. After a minute, he cleared his throat and continued with his story:

"The master had ordered the grounds searched the next morning after he learned Eleanor awoke alone in her room, Lydia's bed not having been slept in. It was a group of riders out hunting by the castle ruins that found the body, hanged by the neck from a smoldering tree."

Richard felt a shiver run down his spine as Frederick said this, the image of the twitching body flashing before his eyes, it's once beautiful face marred by the bulging eyes and the swollen, protruding tongue.

"It so happened," Frederick went on, "that the stablehands, two strong but unsavoury characters the master employed in the spring, had also gone missing that day. Sir Elliot told the authorities that Lydia alleged that the two men had committed an impropriety towards her. Upon learning this, Sir Elliot gave the men notice that their employment would cease, and that they were to be gone by week's end. It was Sir Elliot's belief that, in retaliation for Lydia's accusation, the men administered their own brand of justice by hanging her, then setting the tree ablaze to consume her body. As there was no evidence to the contrary, the authorities accepted Sir Elliot's conclusion, and the incident was not spoken of any further at Elliot House."

"But that's absurd!" exclaimed Richard. "Why display such brutality towards the woman?"

"Because it was the only way to do away with her, a *witch* who cost them their livelihood."

Richard looked at him with a start.

"Yes, master Richard, you heard me correctly, I did say a witch. You see, Lydia's mother was a cunning-folk, a solitary woman who occupied a small cottage by the river, a few miles east of the main bridge. At first, the townspeople went to her for herbal remedies and charms. But rumours soon surfaced that she could perform maledictions as well, a talent reserved for witches, and one that could only be obtained by forming a pact with the devil. It was only a matter of time before the same suspicion fell on Lydia—like mother, like daughter."

"A witch..." said Richard after a pause, recalling the inscription on the label within the curio cabinet 'See through the eyes of a witch'. Looking directly at Frederick, he asked, "Did *you* believe her to be a witch?"

"I did not. And if I may be so bold to add, sir, it is my opinion she encouraged the staff's foolish belief that she was a witch. The association worked to her favour, the servants fearing her and keeping out of her way."

"You make a valid point Frederick," said Richard thoughtfully. "But tell me, what do you believe happened that night. Why did uncle strike her?"

Frederick hesitated a moment before answering.

"From the sound of his voice that evening, he was both shocked and afraid at what she knew. I believe the master struck her for fear of being exposed of some wrong he did the child, and that she died from his blow. Did master intend to kill her? That I cannot say, but there was nothing for him to do but to rid himself of the body, and for this, I believe, he turned to the stablehands. I learned from one of the ground keepers that he had seen Sir Elliot speaking with those men late that evening. My suspicion is that the master paid them handsomely to commit the heinous deed, after which they were to depart the country. They were certainly up to the task—a pair of greedy blackguards who struck me as having no morals, if you will excuse my language, sir."

"And hence the story Uncle Elliot told the authorities," Richard thought out loud. "A pair of superstitious ruffians who murdered out of fear and revenge...

"Tell me," continued Richard after a pause, "Is Lydia's body buried in the church graveyard? I would like to pay my respects."

"Oh no sir, the pastor would not allow the body to be buried on consecrated ground given the accusation of witchcraft. No, you will find her grave at the outskirts of the forest, on our side of the property limits. I will take you there if you wish, sir."

"That won't be necessary Frederick, just steer me in the general direction and I will find it. But first I plan to introduce myself to the pastor, I'll be away a couple of hours at most."

"Very good, sir. Will there be anything else?"

"Just one more question—what has become of Eleanor?"

"She was sent away, sir. Sir Elliot found her employment as a servant at Crawford Manor, not more than five miles from here."

"Thank you Frederick, that will be all."

"Thank you, sir," said Frederick, as he rose to leave. He was at the door when Richard called out:

"By the way Frederick..."

Frederick turned to face Richard.

"Yes, sir?"

"Thank you for your honesty."

"Not at all, sir. I feel the better for it." He gave a slight bow and left the room.

Richard was standing next to an open grave, the smell of damp earth permeating his nostrils. Lydia's pine casket lay next to the grave, having been exhumed by two middle-aged workers hired from the undertaker's office. Yesterday evening, Richard had visited the pastor to convince him that a great wrong had been perpetrated, that Lydia was unjustly accused of witchcraft and denied a proper Christian burial. Richard was most persuasive, and after an hour's conversation the pastor agreed to have the body buried in the churchyard. Richard's offer to donate one thousand pounds towards the repair of the church steeple was also graciously accepted.

"One moment," said Richard as the men were preparing to lift the coffin onto the wagon. "I'll need you to open the casket," he ordered.

The men stared at Richard in disbelief.

"The burial occurred with no witnesses present. It is my duty to ensure the woman's body is in fact present."

The coffin lid was removed, revealing a woman's skeletal frame, some of the bones displaying the blackened scars of fire damage. The skull had broken away from the neck and had come to rest, face-down, upon one of its shoulders.

Covering his nose and mouth with a handkerchief, Richard reached into the coffin and turned the skull over. A sharp gasp came from one of the workers, the other quickly making the sign of the cross. The facial bones were missing, only the hollow, dome-shaped cranium remained, which now rocked slowly from side-to-side within the coffin, just as her body had swayed when it hung from the noose.

What an abomination, thought Richard. *There's no doubt the bone mask came from this poor woman. How did it end up in uncle's cabinet? I can't believe him so evil as to have ordered the desecration of her grave.* Looking over the condition of the body, Richard noticed that some of the fingers as well as a rib were missing. *No, this is not uncle's work. It's far more likely someone familiar with the witch's tale robbed this grave of some of its bones, selling them for a good price as witch's relics. As fate would have it, uncle probably purchased the bone mask at some private sale, not realizing the irony of what he was doing...bringing back in his study that which he paid so dearly to be rid of.*

Richard stood up and addressed the men. "You can hammer the lid back on and take the coffin to the churchyard. The excavated plot should be ready by now." Richard waited until the lid was replaced, then turned and made his way back to Elliot House.

The burial took place at six o'clock that evening. Only Richard and Frederick attended the interment. Frederick had gathered a bouquet of daffodils to place on the grave, which he knew to be Lydia's favourite flower. The two men remained behind after the pastor left, each saying a silent prayer for the woman. It was Richard who broke the silence.

"Dark clouds are looming Frederick. Time to return to the manor before the storm is upon us."

Rubbing the back of his neck while stifling a yawn, Richard pushed aside the legal documents he had been reviewing. *My God,* he thought, *this is as boring as the work I did as a bank clerk. The confounded noise of the rain beating on the windows is hurting my head. I'm for bed.* He rose and took the lamp from the desk, making his way to the door. He slowed as he passed the curio cabinet to look back over his shoulder, then turned and made his way towards it.

"My vision," he said to himself as he stood in front of the cabinet, "it's incredibly sharp and clear once again." His focus was not on the objects within the cabinet, but on the unit itself. There was something off with the engraved design at the base of the unit. He bent down to peer closer while running his finger along the elaborate carvings of serpents, each with open mouth in readiness to swallow the tail of the one in front. There was a fine line two feet from either end of the cabinet where the head of one serpent did not align properly with the tail of its predecessor. He ran his hand along the bottom edge and discovered a slight groove in the wood that traversed the distance between the two points. Richard had stumbled upon a hidden drawer.

A very clever design, he told himself, *there must be a button or catch nearby that springs the drawer open.* He ran his hand along the base of the left-hand side of the cabinet but could feel nothing out of the ordinary. He did the same on the right, but this time his hand stopped a third of the way in. The eye of one of the serpents felt slightly elevated compared to the others. He pressed down on it with his finger and heard a catch release, followed immediately by the sound of a wooden drawer sliding forward. The secret compartment lay partially open. Cautiously, he opened it fully, revealing a single document laying within. It was a legal paper pertaining to his uncle's business. Richard quickly skimmed through it and was surprised to discover the business was a partnership in which Sir Elliot owned but half the business. The other half belonged to Lieutenant Barrett.

"Lieutenant Barrett?" said Richard incredulously, "Frederick was told that the lieutenant was nothing more than a close friend. Yet another deception on the part of Uncle Elliot...but why?"

Richard considered the implications of this for several minutes before returning the document to its compartment, turning it over as he did so. It was then that he noticed writing on the back of the last page. The ink was faded, but there was no mistaking its message. It was a Last Will and Testament. After having perused the page, he once again returned the document to its secret compartment, nodding gravely as he did so.

This won't do uncle, he ruminated. *Lydia was right, you were a thief and I will see to it that your ill-gotten gains are returned to their rightful owner.*

Heading back to his desk, he reached for the servants bell pull. Frederick appeared after a few moments.

"Have the stablehands prepare a chaise for tomorrow morning—the dog-cart will do. I will be away for several hours but should return in time for tea."

"Certainly, sir."

"And have one of the upstairs bedrooms prepared as well. If all goes as planned I will be returning with a young lady who will be staying with us."

A look of understanding crossed Frederick's face as he replied "Of course, sir. I'll make sure she gets the room directly overlooking the flower garden."

Eleanor was seated in the chaise as Richard bid farewell to Sir Crawford. The two men had dined together and had come to an amicable agreement regarding the return of Eleanor to Elliot House, with Richard agreeing to pay Sir Crawford three months wages for the inconvenience her immediate departure would cause the household.

Neither spoke as the horses made their way down the steep lane that led away from the manor. Richard observed that she did not resemble Lydia, which at first he thought odd until he recalled they were not related. Lydia had been fair-skinned with flowing red hair, while the young woman sitting next to him was of a darker complexion with chestnut-coloured hair pulled into a tight bun. A quarter mile out, Richard brought the buggy to a stop and turned to face Eleanor. She continued to look straight ahead as he addressed her.

"Eleanor, I know you must have hated my great uncle for sending you away, but I want to assure you that I am nothing like him, and mean you no harm. Your rightful place is at Elliot House as its mistress, not a servant."

At these words, Eleanor turned to face Richard, a puzzled look on her face.

"If you will allow me," Richard began in a

calm, steady voice, "I will tell you what I think happened on that fateful day when Lydia disappeared."

Eleanor slowly nodded her consent.

"Frederick told me you were responsible for cleaning uncle's study, and I suspect one day, quite by accident, you triggered the opening of the curio cabinet's hidden drawer. It contained a document whose contents probably meant nothing to you, but on the back of the last page you recognized your name amongst the faded writing. As Sir Elliot was away that morning, you decided to take the document to Lydia. You were hoping that she would tell you why your name appeared on that page—"

"But she did not," interjected Eleanor in a soft voice. "Instead, she told me to return the papers to where I found them and to tell no one about them. She promised she would explain later why my name appeared on that page. But she never got the chance... I'm not sure why, but I believe Lydia would still be alive today had I not found those documents. I feel responsible for her death..."

"You mustn't believe that for a moment,

Eleanor. The truth is, it was my uncle who killed her."

Eleanor uttered a startled exclamation as she turned to face Richard, a look of horrified amazement on her face.

"Sir...Elliot" she stammered.

Richard nodded, then looked away for a few moments, affording the girl some time to come to terms with this revelation before he continued:

"Lydia confronted Sir Elliot that evening about the contents of those papers. They not only showed that half the money from the sale of the business belonged to your father, but that he left it all to you. While in hospital, your father wrote a new will on the back of the partnership agreement, and that's why your name appeared there. The will states that you, Eleanor, are the sole beneficiary of his wealth, and that it was Sir Elliot's duty to assign a legal trustee to manage your estate until you reached the age of eighteen, when the entire sum becomes yours to do with it as you wish. Lydia threatened to expose Sir Elliot for the theft of your rightful inheritance, and it was then that he struck her down. Everything that happened afterwards was just an elaborate scheme on my uncle's part to place the guilt on the stable-hands, knowing the authorities would accept his version of the events."

Reaching out and placing his hand softly on her shoulder, Richard added:

"Lydia loved you dearly Eleanor, and she died fighting for what was rightfully yours..."

Eleanor turned away as she wiped tears from her eyes, declaring tenderly "I loved her too..."

Richard removed his hand from her shoulder and took hold of the reins, the two of them sitting in silence for a short time before he cleared his throat and said, in a more cheerful tone, "Come, let us be off now. Frederick must be worried that something has happened to us. He is anxiously awaiting your arrival."

She turned to look at Richard, the tears replaced by a gentle smile. "Yes, let's be on our way," she said softly, "I have missed Frederick terribly."

Frederick was standing by the front door as the chaise drew up to the house. At the sight of

Eleanor, he could not help but smile as he made his way down the front steps.

Poor fellow, thought Richard with some amusement. *I'm sure he has been standing there for quite a while. It's certainly the first time I've seen the old man smile. Like a mother hen he his. Has probably driven the staff half-mad in preparation for her arrival...*

Richard remained seated as Frederick helped Eleanor down from the chaise.

"See to it that she is served tea and sandwiches in the drawing room, Frederick. We were delayed on the way here and I'm sure the young lady must be hungry by now."

"Everything is ready, sir."

"Splendid. As there is nothing pressing that needs our attention today, you can take your time to settle into your home, Eleanor. And please rely on Frederick for anything you may need. I have a previous engagement, but will return this evening..."

"Eleanor is back at Elliot House," said Richard as he placed a daffodil on Lydia's grave. "I will bring her by after Sunday's service. I can tell she misses you painfully. Perhaps having you here will help bring some closure..."

He was interrupted by the sudden caw of a crow. He looked up and saw it circling overhead before landing atop the church steeple. Turning his attention back to the grave, he was surprised to see a woman dressed in mourning approaching him, her face covered by a black veil. She stopped across from Richard, Lydia's grave separating them.

"You have done well, Richard," said the visitor, lifting her veil to reveal a middle-aged woman with fair skin and sleek red hair. "My daughter can safely rest in peace here, at least for the time being."

Richard remained silent.

"Nothing to say? Well, it does not surprise me. I can understand your anger towards me for causing you such pain and terror, but in my defence, a mother will go to any lengths to help her child. As you suspected, I am the one who hexed the bone fragment, knowing curiosity would get the better of you, that you would want to *see through the eyes of a witch*." There was a hint of mockery in her voice as she said these words. "Once a part of Lydia was inside you, I could make you witness the crimes your uncle committed—the murder and desecration of my daughter and the theft of Eleanor's rightful inheritance. But I must say..." she added after a moment's reflection, "I was not expecting you to put right the wrongs of your great uncle."

She had been slowly making her way towards Richard as she spoke, and now stood facing him.

"In addition to being a witch, you should also know that I am a vengeful person. I regret that Sir Elliot passed away so soon after his hunting trip, robbing me of the pleasure of killing him myself. But at least I have the satisfaction of eliminating what remains of his lineage."

Richard had just time enough to comprehend her meaning when she thrust her hand violently into his face, her fingers cutting through his flesh, penetrating deep under his skin. In one powerful, downward pull, she snapped his neck, then wrenched her hand upwards and away from his face as his body fell to the ground. Richard's face remained in her hand, each of her fingers protruding through its flesh. Peeling it free from her hand one finger at a time, as if removing a glove, she tossed the bloody mass aside, then reached down to rip the bone mask away from his exposed skull.

"There, that wasn't too difficult. One step closer to making you whole again, my dear daughter. It should not be difficult to track down the remainder of your bones. Monsters like Sir Elliot kept to elite circles, and the charlatan who sold him the bone mask will have sold your other bones to fellow collectors. In a few weeks I will have gathered them all, and can then begin the task of returning you to this earth. I presume you'll want to be with Eleanor when you're back? A simple spell that will distort her memory will make that possible. I think the three of us would make such a lovely family, perhaps moving abroad, living *la belle vie* in France.

"But I should not get so far ahead of myself. I will need help bringing you back, and the Dark Lord will demand much in return. But you do not need to concern yourself with this Lydia. As I told Richard, a mother will go to any lengths to help her child..."

THE BONE GATHERERS

1860

Dr. Farwell was carefully examining the small, powdery white spots. "I don't like the look of this," he muttered to himself. "No, I don't like it one bit." He ran the leaf several times between his index finger and thumb. "I guess it was inevitable given all the rainfall we've experienced lately." He gave the leaf a sharp tug, snapping it from the stem, then slowly stood up, brushing the garden dirt from the knees of his trousers before straightening his back with some difficulty. "Damn these old bones," he cursed as he rubbed the base of his spine.

"Good morning," came a greeting from over his shoulder. Dr. Farwell turned to see a young man, smartly dressed in a brown-tweed walking outfit, standing by the garden gate. "I must say, I've never come across a Camellia plant with such vibrant, red flowers. Truly an eye-catching beauty," he added.

"Thank you," replied Dr. Farwell with a hint of a smile. "Unfortunately, *Mycosphaerella macrospora* has decided to invade this beautiful specimen."

"*Mycosphaerella...?*" inquired the young man.

"Common powdery mildew. Nothing to do I'm afraid but prune back the infected foliage and hope that it has not spread to the neighbouring plants."

"I'm very sorry to hear that," the young man said earnestly, then added in a slightly more animated tone, "By the way, my name is Godfrey Haworth, terribly rude of me not to have introduced myself sooner. I've recently rented the cottage at the top of Lathrop hill."

"Yes, I know," said Dr. Farwell, "News travels fast in a small village like ours. My name is Dr. Farwell. I was the local physician here for 30 years before I retired last spring, a role now performed admirably by Dr. McBurney, who resides but ten minutes from your cottage."

"It's a pleasure to make your acquaintance Dr. Farwell, and I will be sure to drop by later today and introduce myself to Dr. McBurney."

"He would welcome your company, I'm sure." Then, after a slight pause, added, "Tell me Mr. Haworth, if you don't mind my asking, what brings a young lad like yourself to Crail."

"I don't mind at all. I'm working on a proposal for an expedition to Negev which I hope to present to The Royal Geographical Society next month. A good colleague of mine, Professor Burke, has been carefully mapping the site of Byzantine Shivta in the Negev Desert. He's very eager to begin excavations and has asked me to join his team."

"Sounds like a major undertaking," commented Dr. Farwell.

"It certainly is. I'm rather an enthusiast of biblical archaeology, so I've agreed to join the team and said I would help to raise the required capital. I thought it best to remove myself from the distractions of the city as I focus on that task."

"And hence your stay at Lathrop hill—silence as well as solitude," added Dr. Farwell.

"Precisely."

Dr. Farwell looked down at the leaf he had removed, then added wistfully, "I must say, I do envy you—getting to explore such an ancient and mysterious land. At my age, I find a day's visit to London to be totally exhausting."

"As does everyone else," added Geoffrey, smiling.

Dr. Farwell gave a short laugh, then said, "I know we've just met, and I hope I'm not being too presumptuous by asking, but do you think you could help me in the garden for a minute? I have a rather unruly Corokia hedge whose soil needs tilling, and I need someone to hold back the stems so I can get at the base of the shrubs."

"Think nothing of it, I am more than happy to be of some service. Besides, I'm awfully interested in seeing what other magnificent plants you have blooming beyond this gate."

"Come along then, and I'll give you a quick tour before we work on the hedges. As you can see, it's not a very large garden but it does have some unique features."

It was immediately obvious to Geoffrey that the garden was carefully tended to by its owner. Well-trimmed bushes bordered a meandering gravel path. Plants of different heights and assorted flowers filled the area behind the bushes, providing a wonderful tapestry of colour. There was an ornamental cherry tree in full bloom at one end of the garden, and a lovely rose walk that led to a circular patch of close-cut lawn at the opposite end, where a wooden bench sat facing the cherry tree. Behind the bench and just outside the edged border of the lawn stood a relatively tall, very solid-looking wall of green foliage—the Corokia hedge.

"I really must congratulate you on maintaining such a splendid garden. I will think of it often when I'm enduring the summer heat of the Negev Desert."

"I'm glad to hear it. But now I must put you to work. If you'll just push back as much of these densely packed branches from the base of the hedge, I'll begin to break up the soil with my spade."

The men had worked their way towards the middle of the hedgerow when the tip of Dr.

Farwell's spade turned over a solid object from the soil. Geoffrey reached down to retrieve it. He brushed the loose soil away with his hands and studied it for a minute, a puzzled look on his face. Handing it to Dr. Farwell he said:

"I don't profess to know much about anatomy, but that looks like a bone to me, somewhat deformed in shape, flattened but still intact."

"Yes...I would say your surmise is correct. In fact, this is a human bone, most likely part of the humerus, the bone found in the upper arm. Although flattened, the proximal region can still be made out."

"A human bone—what a grisly find!" said Geoffrey, aghast.

"It's not too unusual to find the occasional bone surfacing in gardens and farmer's fields around here. Many battles were fought and folks buried on this land over the centuries. I'm sure bones will be surfacing for years to come."

"I imagine so. But what about its peculiar shape, crushed flat, as it were, but still in one piece."

Looking the bone over, Dr. Farwell replied after a moment, "I know one person who might have an explanation for that—Reverend Green. He's extremely knowledgeable about the history of Crail and has some very peculiar tales when it comes to explaining the appearance of such bones."

"I'd be curious to hear them."

"Well then, why don't you come with me to the vicarage tomorrow? Reverend Green is expecting me for tea. I'll swing by tonight and let him know that I will be bringing a guest tomorrow, along with a bone for the ossuary!"

Geoffrey laughed. "Invitation kindly accepted," he replied, cheerfully.

The two men continued their work, discussing a variety of topics, including Darwin's work outlining the theory of evolution, and the growing interest in psychical research (a phenomenon both men were highly skeptical of).

When Geoffrey left the garden at midday, he was in high spirits, having found a new, and hopefully lasting friendship in Dr. Farwell. He was looking forward to their visit with the reverend tomorrow. He had a feeling their bone discovery would be the basis of a lively conversation.

The vicarage was a handsome house located at the northern edge of the village, a leisurely thirty-minute walk from Dr. Farwell's home. Reverend Green, an elderly man with a round, jovial face, welcomed them warmly at the front gate before leading them to his study, where tea and scones served with clotted cream awaited them. He motioned to the two empty armchairs in front of his well-polished desk. "Please have a seat gentlemen while I pour us some tea. I cannot tell you how nice it is to have visitors who wish to speak about something other than next week's fete. Not that I mind helping with organizing the affair mind you, but it's dealing with the minutia of each event that I find so tiring. Do you know, Mrs. Wood kept me over an hour yesterday discussing whether we should offer Mrs. Thompson's blueberry pies in the refreshment tent as they did not really 'fit the sophisticated atmosphere' she was trying to convey. I don't mind telling you gentlemen, that Mrs. Thompson makes the best blueberry pies in all of England, and I can't image not having one at the fete. So, I told Mrs. Wood that the pies would be eaten so quickly that in no way would they cause any sort of 'atmospheric disharmony.' Let us hope she values my opinion on the matter!" He delivered this final line as if he were preaching a sermon, hand raised high, index finger pointing to heaven.

After a few more minutes of light discourse on food, the reverend took his seat behind the desk and addressed Dr. Farwell. "But let us not bore your new friend with such trifle stories." Then turning to Geoffrey, added, "You must excuse us Mr. Haworth, we elderly gentlemen do tend to babble on. I must say, I'm so happy you have come. Dr. Farwell brought me a rather peculiar bone last night which the two of you found in his garden." At this point the reverend removed the bone from his desk drawer and laid it on the desk, directly in front of Geoffrey. "I understand you're curious to hear my interpretation of how it acquired its current state."

"Yes indeed, very much so."

"Before I begin my explanation, let me ask you a personal question. Do you believe in Hell, Mr. Haworth? A *physical* place ruled by the prince of darkness—Satan himself."

Geoffrey hesitated for a moment, then answered, "With all due respect reverend, I do not. As far as I'm concerned, Hell is a state of mind, not a place."

"I see...a most sensible answer. Then I'm afraid you'll be most disappointed with my explanation. Nevertheless..." he continued after a moment's reflection, "I think you should hear me out just the same, as there are some aspects of my story I believe you will find interesting."

"I came here because I was anxious to hear your explanation, and I would be most disappointed if I left without hearing it."

"Wonderful! Let me pour you both another cup of tea before I begin."

Having done so, Reverend Green sat back in his chair, rested his elbows on the desk, placed his fingertips together, and began speaking in a clear, yet somber tone:

"In a manner of speaking, you are correct in stating that evil resides within the mind, but the question we need to ask ourselves is, 'who placed the evil there?' Someone, or *something* must corrupt an individual's mind, or soul, so that it contemplates evil in the first place. I put it to you that that something is a *demon*—the disciple of Lucifer.

"Lately, it has become fashionable among the 'psychics and spiritualists' to speak about an invisible veil, one which shields us from an ethereal yet dangerous world that lies beyond ours. Lifting this veil, if it were possible, means certain death or insanity to those who succeed. The human mind simply cannot grasp, and therefore cope with what it sees. I do not believe that such a veil exists, but what I do believe is that a *physical* barrier exists, one that has hindered the passage of demons from entering our world for centuries. Such barriers, or to be more precise, *walls,* are made entirely from human bones."

Here the reverend paused, picking up the bone from his desk. He regarded it for some moments, lost in a deep train of thought, before placing it back on the desk and proceeding with his explanation.

"The walls themselves are found in places where they would be least noticed, in the underground catacombs, ossuaries and charnel houses found across Europe. You see Mr. Haworth, the walls of human bones were erected at locations where demons have tried to burrow through to our world. Obviously the greater populace would be alarmed, to put it mildly, if they discovered such walls, or worse still, if they got it in their heads to see what was on the other side. Hence catacombs—underground labyrinths, sacred sites filled with human bones, stretching for hundreds or thousands of kilometres—were built in the same vicinity as the walls themselves. The presence of so many human bones, many elaborately arranged, perfectly disguised the existence of the bone walls. The catacombs of Rome, Odessa, Vienna and many other cities have been, unbeknownst to most, protecting mankind for centuries."

Geoffrey picked up the bone from the desk and asked, doubtfully, "Are you suggesting that the bone I hold in my hand is from such a wall?"

"Yes, I do. And its compressed shape is the result of thousands of bones being pressed against one another during the construction of the wall itself."

"Thousands of bones being compressed..."

Geoffrey repeated uneasily, then asked, "But who built the walls?"

"Of that I know little," Reverend Green replied. "I've heard that some sacred texts make reference to the *Bone Gatherers*, whose sole purpose is to build and repair the bone walls. Who, or what they are, I do not know."

"But why should such a bone be discovered here in Crail?" Geoffrey pressed the reverend.

"The answer is a simple one Mr. Haworth —we have our own wall, constructed in the fourth century, and located in the catacombs beneath our modest church. Not surprisingly, some bones can fall free of the wall over time. It was probably collected by a priest and kept as a sacred relic somewhere in the church before it burned down in 1708. No doubt it was discarded along with all the other charred debris during its reconstruction. Extensive plowing in this area over decades has likely tossed it from field-to-field dozens of times until it finally came to rest in what is now Dr. Farwell's garden."

"There are certainly a lot of 'ifs' in your explanation, Reverend Green."

"There certainly are, but it remains a reasonable supposition nevertheless. As I said at the start of our conversation, I did not expect you to believe my explanation, but I did say you may find certain aspects interesting, such as this one..."

At this point the reverend reached into the top drawer of the desk and took out a small leather pouch. He gently spilled the contents next to the bone lying in front of Geoffrey.

"I understand you are an enthusiast of biblical archaeology. Perhaps you can tell me something about these items."

Geoffrey carefully picked up the first object. He shot a quizzical look at the reverend and then refocused his attention on the small relic that was now resting in the palm of his hand.

"But this is fantastic..." Geoffrey said, somewhat in disbelief. "This is an ancient bronze cross, with five circles around it representing the five wounds of the Lord Jesus. Dates back to at least AD 600. And this..." Geoffrey replaced the cross on the table and picked-up a coin, "...this is a Gold Solidus depicting Justin II holding a sceptre and cross. I would put the date of this coin circa AD 580. As for the ring..." he now examined the last item on the table, "...it bears an image of a shepherd boy, no doubt symbolizing Jesus as the 'Good Shepherd.' I would date it as early third century."

"Marvelous!" exclaimed the reverend. "Dear sir, your knowledge is impressive indeed. Tell me, would you be interested in helping me identify more of these artifacts? It just so happens that I have an opportunity to collect a few more tonight."

"Tonight? Why certainly I will. When and where are we to meet?"

"Perhaps after evensong would be best. Let us meet at the church, since these artifacts come from the wall in our catacombs." Geoffrey was about to speak when the reverend held up is hand to stop him. "I know you do not believe the story I have just recounted Mr. Haworth, and in no way am I asking you to. Nevertheless, a wall does exist. It's composed of thousands of bones, and you should not be surprised that artifacts, like the ones I've shown you, occasionally find their way into the wall along with the bones of those who acquired them. The wall is now crumbling in one of its corners, and we have the opportunity to collect a few more sacred items from that particular spot. Are you still interested in coming?"

"You could not keep me away if you tried, reverend."

"I'm glad to hear it Mr. Haworth. And I hope you will join us as well Dr. Farwell?"

"It would be an honour. I was just telling Mr. Haworth yesterday how envious I was about his upcoming expedition. In some small way, I now feel as if I'm going on an exotic expedition of my own."

"Then I will see you both around six-thirty tonight. Best to meet by the rear doors so as not to disturb any parishioners who may still be in the church. And now I must bid you a good day gentlemen as I need to prepare for my evening sermon."

The two men arrived at the church slightly before the agreed upon time. Reverend Green was waiting for them just inside the doorway, a lit oil lamp already in his hand.

"This way gentlemen," he said in a hushed voice, "unfortunately I have but the one lamp, so please stay close at all times. The staircase leading to the catacombs is at the end of this corridor to the left, hiding in plain sight, as it were."

Reverend Green led the way down the flight of shallow stone steps, the centre of each worn down by centuries of use. The staircase was narrow, so the men descended in single file, the reverend leading the way with his lantern, which cast an ominous light that danced and leapt on the stairwell wall with each downward step. After a slow, cautious decent, an entrance way was reached. A massive oak door barred the way forward. It was medieval in construction, iron strips applied to its surface with large, round-headed rivets. Reverend Green shot back the large bolt securing the door. Turning to face the two men, he beckoned them to follow.

The subterranean passageway was narrow, no more than a few metres wide. This gave Geoffrey the grotesque feeling that the bones lining the walls and those within its recesses were spilling forth, closing in on him. The oppressive atmosphere made it difficult to breath, as if a *mal'aria* emanated from the very bones themselves.

Truly a sad and awful place, Geoffrey thought to himself.

After several minutes of walking in silence, the reverend stopped and pointed to a set of steps. "We are almost there," he said in a hushed tone. The staircase led to a deeper, much narrower tunnel so that once again the men were forced to walk in single file. After turning into a connecting tunnel, they eventually reached a large chamber.

The reverend held up the lantern so that it illuminated the far wall. "Behold gentlemen, the bone wall that has been keeping evil at bay for centuries..."

Geoffrey looked on in disbelief. A wall composed totally of bones, compressed flat, almost smooth in appearance, stood before him. At first, he thought he might be the victim of an elaborate hoax, that the wall was nothing more than a painting. But when he went to examine it, he could feel the physical contour of the bones, sense its solid presence. He turned and looked at the reverend in awe, asking:

"But how..."

"I knew you would be impressed Mr. Haworth. But as I said this afternoon, I do not know how or who built such a structure, but I thank the Lord it is here to protect us."

Taking Geoffrey by the arm, the reverend led him to one of the corners. "Look here," he said, illuminating the base of the wall. "As I stated previously, the wall has started to crumble at this point. This is where I found the artifacts I showed you this afternoon, amongst the fallen bone debris. The hole itself extends much deeper into the wall. I am hoping you can reach in and clear out any remaining bones that may have fallen. I'm certain we will find a few more important artifacts amongst them."

"Why certainly," replied Geoffrey enthusiastically, "just place the lamp to my left and I'll lie down and reach in." Before doing so, Geoffrey removed a small flat trowel from his trouser pocket.

"Well done, I see you have come prepared," said Reverend Green as he took a few steps back to allow Geoffrey more room to work.

Geoffrey's arm was fully extended into the

hole when the trowel slipped from his hand. *That's queer, I could have sworn it was pulled free from my hand.* No sooner had this thought crossed his mind when something grabbed at his wrist, yanking his arm with such force that his entire body slid forward, causing the side of his face to be pressed painfully against the wall. Geoffrey let out an agonizing yell, tears filled his eyes as he pressed them shut from the pain. Reaching out with his left arm, he shouted in panic, "Help me reverend! Grab my arm, pull me back!" He managed to open one eye and tried to focus. The lamp was gone. The chamber was pitch black. He was in tears as he whimpered "Please...reverend..." Suddenly there was another violent pull on his arm which caused his head to bend so far sideways against the wall that it snapped his cervical spine. Another tug and half his torso was pulled into the narrow opening, his blood and organs spilling outwards.

"Such an awful business...," said Dr. Farwell, still gasping for breath as a result of his hurried return to the catacomb entrance.

"It most certainly is...but sadly such sacrifices...are necessary," responded the reverend, just as winded as Dr. Farwell and wiping the sweat from his brow with a handkerchief. "Every seven years on the day of The Ascension of the Lord, the Bone Gatherers arrive to reinforce our sacred wall—the timing cannot be changed. Unfortunately, the demons have slowly been accelerating the rate at which they chip away at the wall. We cannot have them breaking through before the Bone Gatherers arrive. Thankfully the demons are but savage beasts, and just as we can delay a dog from digging its hole by tossing it a scrap of food, so can we delay the demons from their work by offering them an innocent soul to torment, in this case that of Mr. Haworth. Yes, a most regrettable solution, but one that grants us the extra time needed for the Bone Gatherers to arrive and begin their work."

The men could feel the earth trembling beneath their feet as the reverend spoke his last few words. The Bone Gatherers were making their way toward the wall, pushing thousands of bones forward through their underground network, bones that will form a new layer of wall over the old, a barrier that will help protect humanity from evil for another seven years.

"Ah, they are almost here," said the reverend, closing the heavy oak door and bolting it shut. He made the sign of the cross before adding in a hoarse whisper *'festina cum Deo.'*

"Yes, God speed indeed," repeated Dr. Farwell, before he turned and followed the reverend slowly up the dimly lit staircase.

THE FORGOTTEN KING

1939

The Glendon County Zoo opened its doors to the public on a warm spring day in 1929. It was a small zoo built in the shape of a trefoil, similar to a three-leaf clover. It had secured only thirty animals for its opening, among them an ostrich, two chimpanzees, and one African lion. The limited number of exhibits did not, however, dampen the enthusiasm with which the children of Glendon's public school looked forward to their zoo visit. My grandfather was a boy of 10 then, in Miss. Bennett's elementary classroom, which consisted of 13 children between the ages of six and twelve. "Poor, poor Miss Bennett," grandfather would say, decades later, shaking his head slowly from side to side as he spoke. "She had arranged our field trip to the zoo that morning. How could she have known...how could anyone have foreseen such a tragedy?" One which was to haunt my grandfather for the remainder of his life. After he passed away, I came across his journal in my mother's study. It contained a detailed account of what happened at Glendon County Zoo on that fateful day, as recorded by him a decade later. Though I was already familiar with the story (as was everyone in Glendon County), it is worth retelling. If it were not for the newspaper photo still on display at the zoo, I would not have believed what he wrote. Here is his story.

I had a keen interest in lions from an early age. I believe it started after Mother read *The Wonderful Wizard of Oz* to me. I was a rather timid child and found comfort in the idea that, like the Cowardly Lion, I too could find my courage. But it was not until I came across *Tarzan and the Gold Lion* that I truly become fascinated with the "king of the beasts". The book was lying on the small mahogany table next to the living room armchair—obviously father had been reading it the night before and forgot to replace it on the bookshelf—he most certainly would not have deemed it suitable for a child to view, let alone read. On the cover was an image of a majestic lion, every muscle taut, staring straight ahead, with its mouth slightly ajar. Beside him was Tarzan, spear in hand, ready to join the great beast on its deadly hunt. Of the eight illustrations within the book, one in particular stood out. The Gold Lion was attacking an ape-man, its jaws buried deep in the victim's neck. The sheer brutality of the scene both frightened and fascinated me. Little did I know it was an ominous sign of events to come.

You can image my absolute elation when I learned that a zoo was going to open in our small county and that an African lion was to be one of its exhibits. The grand opening was still four months away, and I counted down the days by drawing a lion's head on our kitchen calendar with each passing day.

About a week before the zoo's grand opening, I came home from school crying. My hopes of visiting the zoo had suddenly been dashed.

Tommy, who sat next to me in class, had learned from his older brother that the cost of admission was to be 10 cents, rather expensive for those days. I feared that when I conveyed this news to father he would reply, in his most authoritative voice: "My dear child, we have more important things to do with our money than visit a zoo." Fortunately, such a conversation did not occur. Miss Bennett, (God bless her kind soul) arranged to have our class visit the zoo at no cost, admission courtesy of the zoo.

After what felt like an eternity, the day finally arrived. I left home at 9:00 a.m. The walk to the zoo would take an hour as it was a good three miles away, located just north of Franklin's creek. The younger children (I can still recall their names—Dorothy, Mary, Virginia, "Little Ruth", Joseph and George) were not required to walk as Mr. Davies, the general store proprietor, offered to drive them in his new vehicle (when the children were told of this, they seemed more excited at the prospect of receiving a ride than visiting the zoo). The class assembled outside the main entrance at the arranged time, and Miss Bennett took a minute to review the "rules of proper conduct" with us: "Stay together at all times, no shouting, be courteous to others, and no feeding the animals." Then with a cheerful smile she motioned us to follow her through the main gate.

Upon entering, we found ourselves in front of a large fountain populated with several varieties of ducks. The ducks captivated the attention of the younger students, so we spent half an hour watching the colourful birds paddle and forage for food before moving on. From there, we followed the main circular path around the zoo, and in little over an hour had seen most of the animals, as several of the exhibits still remained empty. We were approaching the end of our visit and had just turned the corner from the reptile enclosure when, directly ahead, I saw a cage bordered by two wooden cut-outs of palm trees. The sign above the cage read "King of the Beasts". But what I saw inside the cage was no king. The scene deeply saddened my heart.

There, in a twelve-by-ten foot iron cage, the African lion laid sphinx-like in a corner, the shadow from one of the thin cut-outs providing the animal with a narrow band of shade. Its body was thin, the ribcage clearly visible with each breath. Its golden mane looked almost too big for its lean face, and the eyes had a far away, dispirited look. It was utterly disheartening to view such a majestic animal in this state—a prisoner whose view of the world would forever be through the bars of a cage.

There was a guardrail in front of the exhibit, about four feet distance from the cage and three feet in height. Some of the older children decided to sit on top of the railing, while the younger ones swung back and forth below it, all the while imitating the hoots of the chimpanzees they had heard earlier. As I stood there, I noticed a zookeeper approach the cage from the side opposite the lion. He was carrying a small bale of straw for scattering on the concrete floor. He unlocked and partially swung open a small cage door, about three by four feet in size. The lion showed no interest in what he was doing. Without giving it a second thought, I walked over to the zookeeper, pulled on his sleeve, and said, "Excuse me sir."

What a start I gave the poor fellow! He

nearly jumped out of his shoes before turning around and exclaiming, "Sweet Jesus, you're not allowed beyond the railing, it's dangerous!" As he said this, he reached back with his hand and grabbed the open cage door, swinging it shut towards him. Miss Bennett, having heard the zookeeper's exclamation, was now by my side, as was the entire class. The appearance of even more children visibly added to the zookeeper's anxiety.

But Miss Bennett had a friendly, comforting way with people. In a minute she had calmed the zookeeper's nerves, and shortly thereafter had him, somewhat grudgingly, reciting interesting facts about the lion to the children. He concluded by saying, "Now, if you will all follow me, I'll escort you back to the front of the exhibit and, as requested by your teacher, point the way (here he paused slightly to clear his throat) to the public restrooms." The class followed, but after taking a step or two, I turned back to the cage for one last look. I pressed my face against the bars with my hands on either side, and to my utmost astonishment, the small cage door swung forward. The zookeeper had not locked it but simply slammed it shut when I first spoke to him. I jumped back as if the bars where electrified and immediately looked towards the lion—he was up and starting to make his way towards me. I held my breath for a moment, unable to move. One look at the beast's eyes told me this was not the same dispirited animal I had seen a short while ago. His eyes were bright and fierce. The King of the Beasts was ready to hunt.

I heard Miss Bennett call my name, she and the class had walked 15 or 20 yards before noticing my absence. The sound of her voice broke my trance, and I spun and ran to towards her. Even at that distance I noticed a sudden change in her face. Her eyes grew large with the look of terror; her complexion went ashen white. I turned my head to look back as I ran. The lion was out of the cage and moving stealthily in my direction.

"Run children, run!" she shouted, "Everyone scatter!" Some of the children had turned to see the lion approaching, and quickly fled in horror. The younger ones, thinking Miss Bennett was playing a game, ran away laughing, oblivious to the immediate danger. I could feel the ground vibrate under my feet as I ran, the lion approaching with its powerful, heavy strides. I was not five feet from it as it thundered by. It had no interest in me—it had set its sights on a larger prey.

Miss Bennett had turned and was running away from the approaching beast—but her fate was sealed. With a terrific leap the lion pounced on Miss Bennett, digging its two-inch claws deep into her legs, whereupon she stumbled and fell to the ground. Her dress of white muslin turned a crimson red where the lion had struck. She had time to scream only once in agony before the fangs of the beast sank deep into the back of her neck. Keeping hold of its prey between its powerful jaws, the lion headed for a nearby hill next to a service laneway, the body of Miss Bennett leaving a bloody streak on the ground as it dragged between the animal's legs.

Something caught the brute's attention when he reached the hilltop. He was looking down the hill, opposite my direction. He opened his jaws and Miss Bennett's body fell to the ground in a gruesome pose, her neck twisted fully backwards. The beast emitted a thunderous roar and with a violent abruptness charged down the hill and out of sight. There was a moment's silence followed by the sharp crack of a riffle shot. For reason's I still don't fully comprehend, I felt compelled to run and see what had happened (had I not witnessed enough violence for a lifetime?).

At the base of the hill, there was a small gravel parking lot surrounded by two or three maintenance sheds. A pickup truck was the only vehicle in the lot, a few adults had gathered around it. As I approached the scene, I noticed a large streak of blood splattered across the half-open door of the truck, and drops of blood still dripped form the door's mirror. On the ground, a few feet from the truck's door, lay the dead zookeeper on his back, a riffle still clenched in one of his hands. Next to him was the body of the lion, a gaping cavity in the back of his head where a bullet had ripped through. One of the beast's forelegs lay on the zookeeper's bloody chest, where its formidable claws had dug deep into his flesh.

All of us just stared at the horrific scene, too

stunned to do or say anything. The accompanying silence felt deafening but was at last broken when one of the women pointed towards the lion and said in a hoarse, trembling whisper "My God, look at its head!"

The pool of blood around the lion's head was changing, moving in an unearthly manner as it slowly began to mould itself into a recognizable shape. As we continued to watch in disbelief, the man next to me raised his camera and snapped a single photo, a photo which would ensure that this king will never be forgotten. It was published the following day in the *Glendon Chronicle*. I have kept the original newspaper clipping tucked away in father's copy of *Tarzan and the Gold Lion*—a book I will never peruse again.

J. R. Williams, 1939

The Glendon County Zoo has undergone many changes over the years as the number of animal exhibits have grown, the cages being replaced with much larger, naturalistic enclosures. One thing that hasn't changed is the location of the original lion exhibit. The small, rusted cage lies empty, yet it remains one of the most visited exhibits at the zoo. Next to the cage stands a tall sign with an enlargement of a 1929 newspaper article, whose bold headline reads: "TRAGEDY AT GLENDON COUNTY ZOO."

The article recounts the story you have just read, but it includes a single, disturbing photograph of a dead lion. On its head rests a majestic crown. A crown made entirely of blood. A crown fit for a king.

PHANTASMAGORIA

1888

"Phantoms...demons...the living dead. Unearthly creatures that are confined to our darkest dreams...or are they? Tonight, ladies and gentlemen, such spectral nightmares will appear in this very room, prowling about as they hunt...for human souls."

The room was dimly lit with a single table lamp. Professor Lar walked over and stood next to it, continuing: "In a moment, I will extinguish this lamp, and, with the help of my assistant, will begin tonight's phantasmagoria demonstration." He turned the wick down but stopped before the flame was fully extinguished, addressing the audience once more, this time in a grave tone. "Heed my warning. If any of the unholy apparitions you are about to witness attempt to lunge towards you, turn away, as the gateway to a soul is through the eyes. You have been warned, there is little more I can do to protect you..."

Sir Henry shifted slightly in his seat as he leaned closer to Lady Cadogan, saying in a hushed voice, "Such rot. Still, I hear the effects are quite unsettling. If you find any part of the show too intense my dear lady, just tap me on the shoulder and I will escort you out of the room."

Lady Cadogan gave her head a slight nod in appreciation. "Thank you, Sir Henry. And let me be so kind as to extend the same offer to you." A satisfied smile crossed her lips as she detected a faint startled gasp emanate from the pompous man. A moment later, the room went dark.

Soon a nebulous image appeared at the front of the room. It floated closer to the audience, its form becoming clearer as it did so. It spread out its arms and two other apparitions materialized on either side of it, giving Lady Cadogan a start.

She had, like many others in the room, attended phantasmagoria shows in the past, and had found them both thrilling and entertaining. Conventional phantoms, like skeletons and ghosts were projected about the room, looking sinister but not overly frightening. But what hovered in front of the audience now was very different. There was something intensely disturbing about these phantoms. Their faces resembled that of a satyr, the bestial features displaying such concentrated hate the likes of which Lady Cadogan had never before witnessed.

The old fool was right, she thought, *there's something most unsettling about this show.*

The phantoms slowly rose above the audience, moving away from each other as they swayed their heads from side to side, as if searching for their victims. There were several screams as they suddenly lunged down towards the audience, one heading straight for Lady Cadogan. Her heart leaped. She quickly looked away from the approaching terror, a slight breeze brushing her face as the demon passed overhead. From the corner of her eye, she saw that the creatures were once again at the front of the room, heads swaying, rising slowly in preparation for their second attack on the audience. A sense of dread overtook Lady Cadogan. With trembling hand, she reached out and tapped Sir Henry's shoulder.

"Well, what do you think of my idea?" asked Mr. Marting.

"I'm still unclear as to what I am to write about or how much you will compensate me for my time," replied the doctor.

Dr. Wilfrid Anderson was sitting comfortably in the club lounge, leafing through the evening edition of *The Daily Telegraph & Courier*. Across from him sat his good friend, and editor of the newspaper, Mr. Harrison Marting.

"It's really quite straight forward and requires little effort on your part," replied Mr. Marting. "Once a week you submit a single column—a mere two-hundred words in length—on some health-related topic. You may, for example, discuss the best way to treat a headache, review the latest tonics for stomach ailments, or debunk ineffectual cold remedies. By the way, did you know that last year Lady Grace recommended some ghastly formulation of mustard plaster that did little to relieve my cold but did an exceptional job at blistering my skin. I still carry the scars to this day."

Dr. Anderson gently shook his head in the negative. "You are so gullible Harrison, especially when it comes to taking advice from wealthy young ladies."

"That may be so, but your column will be of great interest to our readership, of that I am certain. Now, on the topic of compensation...I'm afraid there is none."

Dr. Anderson looked up from the paper and gave Harrison a hard stare.

"My dear fellow, just think of the new patients I will be sending your way. In fact, if you were not my best friend, I would have to charge you a considerable premium for such prominent advertising in our paper."

Dr. Anderson could not help but smile. He folded the paper and tossed it across to his friend. "Very well, I'll commit to writing six articles initially. If I do not see at least as many new patients at the end of that period, my journalistic endeavour comes to an end."

"Splendid! You truly are a wonderful chap. Can you have the first draft to me by—"

"Dr. Anderson?" interrupted a portly gentleman who stood a few feet away. Neither man had noticed him approach.

"Yes, I'm Dr. Anderson."

Advancing a few more steps, the gentleman said: "Please pardon my interruption, doctor. You may not remember me, but I had the pleasure of meeting you a few weeks ago at a charity event held by Lady Cadogan. We both bid on the landscape painted by her niece, Marie Wright. My name is Henry Ward."

"Why of course, how rude of me not recognize you, Sir Henry. Let me introduce you to Mr. Marting, my good friend and editor of *The Daily Telegraph & Courier*."

"A pleasure to meet you Mr. Marting. I am an avid reader of your newspaper."

"I'm very glad to hear it, Sir Henry. It's a pleasure to make your acquaintance."

Sir Henry bowed slightly then stood hesitating, unsure how to proceed.

Dr. Anderson raised his eyebrows inquiringly

at Sir Henry and asked: "Is there anything I can assist you with, Sir Henry?"

"Yes, it concerns Lady Cadogan..." Again, he gave a slight hesitation before turning towards Mr. Marting. "Please do not think me rude, Mr. Marting, but this is a delicate matter, one which I would prefer to discuss with the doctor in private."

"Not at all my dear fellow. Please take my seat while I go and enjoy a cigar in the smoking lounge."

"Thank you for understanding."

Once seated, Sir Henry began, somewhat tentatively, "Dr. Anderson, I am very worried about the health of Lady Cadogan. She is not well, and the circumstances leading to her ill health are...let us say...rather peculiar. I've come here today in hopes that you would kindly give me your opinion on the matter."

"Most certainly. But you must be aware," added the doctor cautiously, "that I am not her physician, and so may not be in a position to shed much light on what ails the lady."

"Understood. It would be most unreasonable for me to expect any kind of diagnosis on your part." Leaning slightly forward in his chair, Sir Henry said in a somber tone: "Tell me doctor, have you ever attended a phantasmagoria show?"

Dr. Anderson was taken slightly aback by his question. "I have attended one or two shows in the past...but I fail to see what this has to do with Lady Cadogan's health."

"I'm not sure...that is why I am seeking your opinion. You see, a fortnight ago I accompanied Lady Cadogan to a show produced by a Professor Lar. The projected phantoms were quite disturbing in appearance, so much so that Lady Cadogan asked to leave after the first ten minutes."

"Forgive me for saying so," interjected the doctor, "but I find it difficult to believe that a projected image could appear so frightening, especially in view of how common magic lantern shows have become in this day and age."

"It's more than just their appearance that was frightening," replied Sir Henry. "The demon images floated over the audience before diving towards an individual. One specter targeted Lady Cadogan, who said she felt it brush against her face as it passed overhead—I cannot say if she truly experienced this or simply imagined it. In either case, the experience so disturbed her that she asked to leave immediately afterwards. She really was quite shaken. I noticed that her hands were trembling when I accompanied her to her door that evening. Naturally I felt it my duty to call upon her the following morning to see how she was feeling. Her maid told me that her lady was feeling under the weather and was not accepting visitors. I pressed the servant for more information, who admitted that her lady was in a bad way. She did not sleep at all that night and appeared very weak and pale in the morning. The houseboy had been sent to notify her physician who was expected to attend to her later that afternoon. When I returned that evening, I was told I could not see Lady Cadogan, her physician insisting that she rest undisturbed in bed until he ordered otherwise.

"Yesterday, I decided to pay another visit to the household, having been turned away on several occasions these past two weeks. I found her maid beside herself with worry. She is convinced that her lady is dying and that her physician can do nothing to help her. I'm aware I started today's conversation by asking for your opinion, but what I really desire is for you to pay a visit to Lady Cadogan. I know from my previous conversations with her that she holds you in high esteem—you are a physician to several of her closest friends, all of whom speak very highly of your expertise and caring nature.

"Dr. Anderson," continued Sir Henry earnestly, "I care for Lady Cadogan very much, so much so that I hope one day she will be my wife. Something is very wrong with her, and I am totally in the dark as to what that is, as is her physician. I hope you will agree to see her, and I confess that I have been so presumptuous as to arrange it with her maid to expect you tomorrow afternoon."

Dr. Anderson let out a sigh as he leaned back in his chair for a moment's reflection. "What you are asking me to do, Sir Henry, is highly unusual, as the acting physician has not requested my help. Nevertheless, the rapid decline in Lady Cadogan's health worries me a great deal. I will visit her as a concerned friend, and as I will be coming directly from attending one of my own patients, I will conveniently have my medical bag with me…"

The visit did not occur. Early the next morning, Lady Cadogan passed away.

"What do you make of her death?" asked Mr. Marting the next day, having placed the newspaper with Lady Cadogan's obituary on Dr. Anderson's desk.

"In all honesty, I'm not sure what to make of it," the doctor replied, motioning for his friend to take a seat across from his desk. "I had a conversation with her physician this afternoon, a Dr. Bishop. I don't know him personally, but he is well respected in our profession. Graduated top of his class from London University, and many of his patients are prominent people who grace the pages of *Who's Who*."

Mr. Marting gave a low whistle. "Impressive. And what did the esteemed doctor have to say about Lady Cadogan's illness?"

"That he is unable to determine the cause of death. All he could say was that she withered away at an alarming rate, not responding to any of the treatments he administered. It was as if her entire body was undergoing a rapid mortification, a degeneration, if you will."

'Poor woman. She must have suffered horribly."

"Yes, I imagine so. Her doctor told me that not even morphine helped with her pain during her final hours."

"If you don't mind my asking," said Mr. Marting after a pause, "how did Sir Henry come to learn about her illness in the first place?"

"The night she took ill they had been attending a phantasmagoria show—"

"Professor Lar's?" interrupted Mr. Marting.

"The very same. Sir Henry said that Lady Cadogan was so disturbed by the phantom images that she requested to leave after a few minutes. She was visibly shaken when he bid her goodnight at her door, and learned the following day that she had taken ill overnight. He never saw her afterwards, as her physician forbade any visitors. And that, I'm afraid, is everything I know of the matter. I must admit that I feel sorry for the old man, he told me he loved the woman and was hoping to marry her."

"Sad indeed..." Mr. Marting said absently. "Look here," he added suddenly, "you say she attended Professor Lar's show prior to her illness...now that is curious..."

Doctor Anderson gave his friend a quizzical look. "How so?" he asked.

"I'm preparing an article on his show for the paper. Previous to London, he performed in Edinburgh for six weeks, so I interviewed some of the socialites who had attended those shows. All agreed that the performance was truly frightening and at times down-right unnerving. All, that is, but for a certain Sir James..."

"And what did he think of the spectacle?"

"He had no opinion. He died sometime after attending the show..."

A vague sense of unease crept upon the doctor. "I see..." he said slowly, "and if I'm interpreting your journalistic suspicions correctly, you find these deaths a little too coincidental."

"Purely conjecture on my part, of course, but you must admit it warrants further investigation. Two wealthy individuals pass away shortly after attending Professor Lar's show..."

"It is curious, I must admit. However, Sir

James could have died of perfectly natural causes, or had been suffering from some previously diagnosed ailment."

"True, and that is why I will send one of my juniors to Edinburgh to inquire about the cause of his death. I will have his findings by tomorrow morning." The doctor was about to speak but Mr. Marting stopped him short by adding: "And there is no need to ask...of course I will let you know about his findings. In the meantime, I would appreciate if you will accompany me when I interview Professor Lar later today. You are a man of science and may be better able to interpret some of the technical jargon he's bound to use when explaining his equipment. Besides, you would hound me all day for my latest developments on this story, so I may as well have you along."

"You know me too well, my dear fellow. You can depend on my being there."

They met the professor at the home of Sir Richard, an industrial magnate well known in polite society for hosting extravagant masquerade balls. The professor was standing at the front entrance of the three-story Georgian manor. His slim figure stood next to one of the tall Tuscan Columns that framed the doorway, making him look much shorter than his true stature of six feet.

"So glad to meet you both, and thank you Mr. Marting for your paper's interest in my phantasmagoria show," the professor said cheerily. "Please follow me to the East Hall where my equipment is set-up for tomorrow's performance."

As they made their way to the room, Mr. Marting asked: "Tell me professor, why do you choose to perform in private residences as opposed to theatres?"

"A private residence lends an authentic atmosphere to the experience. Do you know of a manor that does not have a ghost or gruesome event associated with its past? Why, this very house is said to be haunted by ancestors of Sir Richard, known to have held devilish rituals in the cellars directly below us. It is just such tales that prime the audience with a feeling of unease or an expectation of fear when they attend my show. This could not be achieved in a theatre venue."

They arrived at a set of elegant double doors whose handles were encircled by a light chain secured by a small padlock. Removing a key from his pocket, the professor continued: "I always keep this room locked. Should Sir Richard or one of his guests enter ahead of time, the entire illusion would be spoiled. It would be the equivalent of entering by the backstage of a theatre and seeing all the pulleys and ropes as opposed to the wonderful effects they produce at the front of the stage."

They entered a room that was fifty feet in length and of high ceiling. A number of magic lanterns were carefully arranged at one end of the room, surrounded on three sides by black curtains that hung from a sleek metal frame that encased the area. Near the centre of the room were twenty chairs arranged in four rows, their backs facing the magic lanterns. Strategically located throughout the forward section of the room, and hanging from different heights, were projection screens made of a thin gauze-like material. Several were attached to pulleys that rested on thin wires that ran the entire length of the room.

Professor Lar looked over at his guests and beamed with satisfaction as he saw the expression of wonderment on their faces.

"As you see before you, gentlemen, several of the screens are attached to pulleys so that any image projected onto them can be made to move towards or away from the audience. Behind you are the magic lanterns we employ. I have perfected a variable focus projector lens with nearly perfect optics. When coupled with a unique carousel mechanism, also of my invention, different images can be rapidly overlaid, producing the illusion of animation, albeit limited in nature. Of course the audience sees none of this equipment when entering the room, as the room itself is in total darkness except for a single lamp lit near the front row. The spectators are escorted individually to their seats by one of my assistants, who remains available throughout the show should anyone wish to leave early."

"I see..." said Mr. Marting, giving the doctor a quick glance before once again addressing the professor. "Do you mind if the doctor and I take a closer look at the magic lanterns?"

"Not at all, right this way gentlemen. I'm sure you'll appreciate some of their subtler intricacies once you examine the equipment for yourself."

Dr. Anderson was not particularly interested in the 'subtler intricacies' of the units, but feigned interest while taking the opportunity to observe the professor more closely.

There's something off about the man, he thought. *His tone is a jovial one, but there is a disturbing undertone to his voice...almost animalistic in nature. In fact, his entire appearance has a subtle beast-like appearance. Hunched shoulders, slightly pointed ears, large, dark-coloured pupils—*

"Congratulations on your innovations, professor. Truly impressive," complimented Mr. Marting, interrupting the doctor's thoughts. "Can we witness an actual demonstration? I believe the high intensity limelight you employ is of sufficient strength to project an image onto a screen despite the brightness of the room."

"That is correct, Mr. Marting. My slides are kept in the mahogany box on the table located directly behind where the doctor is standing now." The professor came over to Dr. Anderson's side and lifted the lid of the elongated storage box. Within, lay about fifty glass slides, each numbered and neatly placed within a grooved slot. He carefully removed the first slide and held it towards the doctor, who gave a shudder when he saw the bestial image etched upon it. *Truly a manifestation of evil,* he thought.

The professor had noticed the doctor's reaction. "Horrible little devil, isn't he? He was among some sketches a friend of mine had created for a play concerning good versus evil that regrettably was never produced. I was helping him clean out his office last year and he offered them to me. They are now the main attraction of my show."

As the professor busied himself inserting the slide into one of the magic lanterns, the doctor turned his attention back to the slide box, wishing to examine it contents further. A folded sheet of paper at the rear of the box caught his attention. Believing it to be an index for the slides, he examined it. The doctor gave an involuntary shiver as a sketch of the demon stared up at him. Written along the margin was *Das Buch Dunkelheit, 1496.*

"A most frightening image, professor," said the doctor, replacing the paper and turning to face the image the professor was now projecting on one of the screens. "I can only imagine the effect it has on the audience within a darkened room, especially when animated."

"Yes, I'm very proud of the effect. But you and Mr. Marting must come to my show to-morrow night. Surely you could not complete your article without seeing it first, is that not so Mr. Marting?"

"Quite so, professor. You can rest assured we will be there. But the doctor and I must be on our way, for I fear we've taken up a consider-able amount of your time as it is. Thank you again for receiving us." Making for the door, Mr. Marting added: "No need to trouble your-self professor, the doctor and I can find our own way out. Good day."

Once seated in the carriage, Mr. Marting waited for the footman to shut the door before addressing his friend. "The professor is no fool, that much is apparent."

"He most certainly is not," replied Dr. Anderson. "Quite an elaborate production he has created. But I must be frank, I don't like the man and I believe him to be a liar."

"A liar?" said Mr. Marting, surprised by his friend's assessment. "How so? I found him very forthcoming with his answers to our questions."

"True, but he lied about the source of the demon images. I found a sheet within the slide box that referenced a volume of the date 1496 entitled '*Das Buch Dunkelheit*'

"The Book of Darkness..." murmured Mr. Marting.

"I am acquainted with an antiquarian who owns a sizable collection of incunabula dealing with witchcraft and diabolism," said the doctor. "I think I will pay him a visit tonight. He may be familiar with the book in question."

" Yes, let us hope so..." said Mr. Marting pensively. "Why don't we meet tomorrow afternoon at the club before attending the professor's show—let us say half-past five? I will have heard from my junior correspondent in Edinburgh by then. Perhaps we will be in a better position to make sense of these deaths and if they are in any way connected to the professor. In some way I feel I have made a mountain out of a mole-hill over Lady Cadogan's untimely death."

"Let us hope you are right and that there is nothing sinister at play here," the doctor said cautiously, trying to dismiss the sense of fore-boding slowly encroaching on the back of his mind.

By the time the two men arrived at the club, the afternoon had turned gray with heavy rain clouds. They found the library vacant but dimly lit, so seated themselves next to one of the windows.

"I see..." said Dr. Anderson after listening to Harrison's report, "Sir James passed away within a week of attending the professor's show and the cause of death is unknown, as was the case for Lady Cadogan..."

"It appears so. And what news do you bring—did you have an opportunity to meet with your antiquarian friend?"

"I did. He informed me that a copy of the

book can be found in the Bibliotheca Palatina at Heidelberg University. He has studied it himself, as it is written in vernacular German, and therefore easily understood. There is no doubt that the demon renderings used by the professor come from this book. The demons themselves are a thoroughly nasty lot, having been placed on this earth by the devil himself to commit heinous deeds against mankind. The violence behind their deeds is said to increase gradually over the years, so that we become habituated to, and hence complacent with the growing corruption they inflict on our world.

"Not surprisingly," continued Dr. Anderson, "the demons must take on human form if they are to walk freely among us. They accomplish this transformation after 'stealing' the souls of at least three people, each of whom 'wither away' in a painful death afterwards, the third victim suffering the most. The text also notes that those most susceptible to this horrible fate are individuals that possess the ability to see the demon for what it is—a manifestation of pure evil..." At this point the doctor winced in pain and leaned slightly forward in his chair.

"What is the matter?" asked Mr. Marting in alarm.

"I fear," the doctor said unsteadily, "these past couple of days have affected me quite badly. I awoke this morning feeling weak and in pain. I took a restorative but my strength continues to abandon me with each passing hour. I should tell you that yesterday, when I viewed the demon image, the first thought that passed my mind was that it was the embodiment of pure evil. As a man of science I have great difficulty in believing in devils and demons, but I must admit something very queer is happening here. Either they do exist and the professor, intentionally or otherwise, has conjured them up through his unique apparatus, or he himself is a psychopath. Perhaps his mind has been diseased by that cursed book and he is poisoning his victims in some unobserved manner, taking on the role of the demon himself."

The doctor let out a long sigh as he closed his eyes and leaned back in his chair. There was a note of despair in his voice as he added: "Unfortunately, I suspect the former explanation to be the more likely one. Let us hope to God I am mistaken..."

"Damn it all, man!" exclaimed Mr. Marting as he reached out and grabbed the doctor's arm firmly. "Do not for one second entertain such thoughts. There is nothing supernatural happening here. The best action to take now is to go and confront the professor with what we know. By God, I'll get the truth from the professor if I have to beat it out of him!"

An hour later the two friends found themselves once again at the home of Sir Richard. They were shown to the library by the butler, who informed them that "the professor is occupied in the main hall preparing for tonight's show. I will let him know you are here."

"Please tell him to hurry," added Mr. Marting anxiously, "We are at risk of missing our publishing deadline unless he can provide clarification on a few technical details before the start of the show."

"Certainly, Sir. I will convey the urgency of your message."

The men remained silent as they paced the

room impatiently while awaiting the professor's arrival. It was Dr. Anderson who spotted the leather-bound volume with metal clasps resting on a small side table. He made his way to it and stood looking at the book in silence for a moment or two. Then, with increasing apprehension, he reached down and turned over the front cover.

"*Das Buch Dunkelheit,*" he murmured to himself, feeling a slight tightening of the throat as he read the title on the inside page. Keeping his back to the room, he said in as loud a tone as he could muster, "Harrison, over here...quickly."

But his call went unheeded. Mr. Marting had taken but a single step before falling to his knees. His head spun and he could scarcely breath, an oppressive atmosphere having permeated the room. He looked on in horror as the room suddenly darkened and a shadowy outline materialized next to the doctor.

A horrific scream shattered the silence as streams of fluorescent light poured forth from the doctor's eyes. They flowed towards the spectral shadow, drawn into its darkness. The shadow became increasingly darker as it took the light in, changing in appearance as it did so, from that of a bestial demon to one of a man.

*Dear God, it's stealing his soul...*Harrison thought in horror.

Moments later, the darkness receded. Dr. Anderson's twisted body lay on the ground, nothing more than a skeletal frame covered by desiccated flesh. Next to the body stood a well-dressed gentleman with cane and top hat. His coal-black eyes appeared to glisten as he gave a low, almost inhuman laugh. He tipped his hat toward Mr. Marting's kneeling body, then walked slowly across the room and out the door.

Mr. Marting did not go home that evening, nor will he ever do so again. He now resides in the Broadmoor Asylum for the criminally insane. On that fateful night he took a poker from the fireplace of Sir Richard's library and proceeded to smash the equipment used for the production of the phantasmagoria show. When Professor Lar attempted to stop him, Mr. Marting bludgeoned him to death with the poker, administering no less than twenty blows to his head. He gave no reason to the authorities for his actions, as he knew no one would believe that his act of violence was that of a perfectly sane man. His only regret was that he had administered it too late... What walked out of Sir Richard's home that evening was a manifestation of satanic evil in the guise of a gentleman. History will give this man many names, all of which will leave an abiding horror on humanity, including the name that now dominates the headline of every newspaper in England...that of *Jack The Ripper*.

A CHILDHOOD HAUNTING

1981

"Well, here we are," Barbara began quietly, "a visit that has been long overdue. You have haunted my dreams far too often these past twenty years."

Barbara was addressing a vacant, split-level suburban house. As in her dreams, the front door was wide open, inviting her in.

No turning back now, she told herself. *You should have gotten this over with years ago...*

The interior had changed little since she had last played here as a child of seven, the house having maintained its 1960's aura. A spacious dining-room with parquet tiles was the first room off the entrance way. An exposed stone fireplace dominated one wall. On either side hung black-velvet paintings, one of a tall sailing ship, the other of a cascading waterfall in a forest with a deer standing on a boulder. A sectional couch with orange seat cushions was arranged in an "L" shape near the fireplace. Smoked glass-topped coffee tables dotted the room, along with a few plastic palm plants in earthy ceramic pots. A thin layer of dust was visible on many of the surfaces.

Nothing's changed. Everything as I remember it...everything as it appears in my dreams.

Opposite the fireplace wall was the entrance to the kitchen, with its orange wood cabinets and Formica counter. From her favourite spot on the couch, Barbara recalled how she would watch mother in the kitchen preparing dinner.

The kitchen...I always end my dream frantically trying to hide in one of the cupboards...

Barbara turned her attention to a kitchen cabinet located below the counter, next to the refrigerator. She opened the cupboard door and gave a gasp of surprise...

My childhood teddy bear...how could I have forgotten? I tried hiding in the cupboard, but there wasn't enough space for me to fit, so I told teddy to stay there while I desperately tried to find another hiding spot...

She gave the bear a tight squeeze before replacing it in the cupboard.

Upstairs...time to go upstairs and come to terms with what happened there on that fateful day.

The kids' room with its two single beds was located to the right of the landing. Barbara hesitated for a moment outside the room, then turned her attention down the hall towards the master bedroom. She took a long, slow breath, then sat crossed legged on the hall floor and started to replay in her mind the events of that morning:

Every Saturday I would treat mom and dad to breakfast in bed. A muffin for dad and just coffee for mom. When I entered the bedroom that morning with the breakfast tray, I sensed something was different. The room was darker as the curtains were drawn. But mom and dad always left both the curtains and window open—why the exception this morning? And why had they pulled the sheets so high as to cover their faces—surely the room was dark enough with the curtains drawn? I placed the small breakfast tray on the dresser opposite the window and went to stand next to the bed.

I called out to them, but they didn't stir. I took hold of the sheet, and in one swift movement, pulled it off their faces. Blood...blood soaked deep into the sheets and pillows. They had been decapitated. And in an act of perverse terror, their heads had been switched for one another. Father's head rested on what remained of mother's neck, while mother's head had fallen free when I had pulled the sheets away, and now lay face down on father's chest...

I screamed and ran to my room. Teddy was on my bed. I grabbed her and ran downstairs. I must hide, someone is in the house. The kitchen cupboard, but I can't fit, so I leave teddy hidden there, promising I'll come back to get her...

"Barbara, it's time for tea dear."

Barbara looked up with a start. She could hear her mother coming down the hallway, the floorboards creaking under her worn terry-cloth slippers. A moment later she appeared at the doorway, stopping to look down at her daughter, surprised to see that she was sitting crossed-legged on the floor. A warm smile crossed her face as she took a few steps into the bedroom.

"Why dear, are you looking at your old doll house? You stopped playing with it suddenly one day when you were eight...or was it seven...years old? And here you are now, twenty years later, sitting in front of it just like you used to do all those years ago. It warms my heart to see you there again. Good thing I didn't let your father throw it out. I always hoped one day you would bring it home."

"Thanks mom. I'm glad you kept it." Barbara placed her hand gently on her rounded belly. "I'm sure Amy will love it."

Her mother walked over to Barbara and bent down to kiss her head. "I'm sure she will, dear. Father will bring it over to your place next week—whenever it's convenient for you. Now, let me give you a hand getting up and let's head downstairs before the tea gets cold."

As they made their way to the door, her mother stopped and asked: "I don't mean to pry dear, but why did you slap your brother with such force earlier? His cheek is still looking a little swollen."

"Just payback for something wicked he did as a child to my dollhouse some twenty years ago... something that has haunted my dreams ever since. But I'm finally over it now. And don't look so worried mom, you can rest assured that I still love the delinquent."

"I'm glad to hear it dear."

They were about to step out of the room when Barbara held up a finger and said: "One moment, I forgot to do something."

Heading back to the dollhouse, she bent down on one knee and removed the small plastic teddy bear from the kitchen cupboard, placing it next to the girl figurine lying on the bed. "Sleep well," she whispered softly. Then added: "And pleasant dreams...to the both of us."

A SOULFUL PARTING

....

She visits me at midnight
With her melancholy face tilted downwards
over the grave
Mourning my loss, she possesses the tender
reflection that once belonged to me
Darkness wraps me in a clean shroud
A suffocating fate greets me
Warmly, that is
As I watch myself walk away

—Isabel Sloane Tallevi

THE CRIMSON OAK

1972

He sensed the room had brightened and this stirred him awake. Staring down at him, with a mischievous grin on her face, was the bright face of his young teenage daughter, who had just opened the blinds in his room.

"I slept in, didn't I?

"That you did," she replied. "Unless, of course, your plan was to get up this very minute and drive me to school in your pyjamas."

She giggled at her own remark and then straightened herself, shifting her backpack into a more comfortable position as she did so.

"Give me five minutes Lizzie and I'll be ready."

"Oh no you won't," she replied, placing her

hand firmly on his shoulder as he began to sit up. "I know you've been up most of the night working dad—I can hear the tippy-tap of the typewriter keys through my bedroom wall. I still have time to catch the school bus. You take your time getting up. Older people need their sleep."

Once again, a mischievous grin appeared on her face.

"Good one, Lizzie. You definitely have your mother's sense of humour."

Her grin slowly faded away at these words. She hesitated, then added in a soft voice "Dad, today is October 25th."

"I know, sweetheart." He reached out and stroked her cheek softly.

"Mom passed away four years ago today," she continued, then lowered her gaze before adding "I still miss her dad."

"So do I Lizzie, so do I…"

She leaned over and gently kissed his forehead before turning towards the door. She got halfway across the room before adding in a more cheerful tone "This year I decided to wear the hair ribbon she gave me for my 9th birthday." A silky, emerald-green ribbon was tied around her braided ponytail, which she now swayed from side to side. "Beautiful, isn't it?"

"It most certainly is. I'm glad you're wearing it.

"And Lizzie," he added hurriedly.

She turned to face him.

"I'll pick you up after school, OK? Tell Grace I can give her a lift home as well."

"Thanks dad, see you then."

He continued to stare at the empty doorway long after she left for school.

A cold shower helped to lift his spirits and focus his attention on what needed doing that morning. He had lingered in bed far too long, reliving the events that led up to his wife's death. An icy road, a fallen tree branch, a swerving vehicle, a beautiful woman out for a walk, a policeman at the door...

"Let it go, Richard," he said quietly to himself. "Focus on being a good dad to Lizzie— it's all you can do for Caroline now."

He made his way to the kitchen and prepared a coffee. It wasn't until he was returning the milk to the refrigerator that he noticed

Lizzie's lunch on the bottom shelf. *So much for being a good dad,* he scolded himself. Placing the lunch on the counter, he reached for the phone receiver next to the cupboard. Lizzie had taped a folded note to the rotary dial. It had two items listed: *Dad, can we (1) get a push button phone (Grace's family just got one) and (2) say hi to Aunt Kimberly for me.*

He smiled as he placed the folded note in his shirt pocket. "Dialing Aunt Kimberly now..." he said out loud to himself.

She answered after the first ring. "Hello big brother."

"Hi sis—guess you were expecting my call."

"It is October 25th Richard, and my good brother always calls to confirm that we'll meet for coffee at Caroline's favourite diner in honour of her memory."

"A small change of plans this morning if it's OK with you. Lizzie forgot her lunch, so I'd like to drop it off at her school later this morning. Can we meet closer to her school? Perhaps we can stroll along Oak Creek—Caroline loved taking walks there. I'll bring the coffees."

"Sounds like a great idea. It's a beautiful day for a stroll."

"Excellent, meet you at the small parking lot just off Campbell Street around eleven."

"See you then, Richard."

"And Richard," she added with a note of hesitation in her voice "How's Lizzie doing today?"

"She's good sis—she's a resilient young girl. She sends her best and looks forward to having you over for dinner tonight."

"I'm glad to hear she's doing fine. See you soon."

He spotted Kimberly's car parked askew near the confines of the parking lot. *Good old sis,* he said to himself, *she never could back-in properly.*

She was waiting for him a few feet away, next to a path that led to the open park area of the creek. She wore a rainbow stripped V-neck sweater, a recent birthday gift from Richard. "Looks good on you," he remarked. "I definitely have good taste in gifts." She smiled and gave him a hug. He handed her one of the coffees, then raised his cup and said "Here's to you, my beautiful Caroline."

"To Caroline," replied Kimberly. She slipped her arm through his, and they started down the path.

After a short while, Kimberly stopped to point at an oak tree near the creek's bank. "Take a look at that tree Richard...it's beautiful! The leaves are such a vivid red, when they sway in the wind it gives the illusion that they're on fire."

"Ah yes," he replied, "that's the dreaded Crimson Oak."

"Dreaded?" she asked.

He looked at her in surprise. "Surely you must know about it. Don't you remember the rhyme the boys would chant whenever they wanted to scare the girls on the playground? I can still recall it."

> *Oh little girl*
> *Get away from that tree*
> *For a bough it will grow*
> *with the blood from thee*

"Richard!" exclaimed Kimberly "That's absolutely dreadful. Why would they say such a thing?"

"Apparently," he said, "there is an unsettling story behind it. And, I may add, one in which some people believe is true, though they're not likely to admit it."

She stared at him with wide eyes. "Well, go on."

"Do you see the five lower branches on the tree, how they stand out from the others because of their neat circular alignment around the trunk."

"Yes," she answered. "Now that you point it out, it's quite apparent."

There was a moment's silence and Kimberly turned towards her brother. He was staring very intently at the tree, with a puzzled expression on his face.

"Richard?" she inquired.

He blinked and then turned to face her. "Sorry sis," he said absently "I just got caught up looking at the tree. I thought—well never mind. Where were we?"

"You were going to tell me about the five

branches," she said, steering him back to the topic at hand.

"Ah yes. Well, the growth of each of those branches coincided with the disappearance of a young girl. Five girls have gone missing over the past 30 years, and the growth of each branch occurred on the day a girl went missing."

She looked at him in disbelief. "Richard, you don't actually believe that nonsense, do you? Sounds just like the stuff that old wives' tales are made of. Is the tree supposed to walk around on its roots and find a girl to eat?"

"Not quite," he replied with a chuckle. "But I can tell you that the tale has some basis in fact. A few years ago, a well known crime author—last name was Blackwell I believe..."

"Chris Blackwell?"

"That's it—Chris Blackwell—he came to investigate the disappearances for a true-crime book he was writing at the time. He became so obsessed with the story, that he ended up spending two months right here in Port Hope, scouring the newspaper archives for photos of the Crimson Oak taken around the time of the disappearances. He followed this up with ads in the local newspapers, asking folks to submit any photos they had where the tree was visible. Given its brilliant colour, you can image how often the tree gets photographed. In the end, he found several photos that supported the Crimson Oak legend—no branch the day before a girl's disappearance, a new branch clearly visible the day after. His book is in the library if you're interested." He delivered the last statement with a wink.

"No thank you. Think I'll stick to reading Jonathan Livingston Seagull—lots of blue sky and no trees."

"Wise decision," agreed Richard.

No more was said about the Crimson Oak for the remainder of their stroll. At noon, Kimberly said she would stay on a while longer and enjoy the fine weather while Roger left to drop off Lizzie's lunch at her school.

Several teenagers were standing next to the front doors of the school. A tall, lanky boy wearing a Grateful Dead t-shirt opened one of the doors for Richard as he approached.

Richard thanked the boy and flashed a peace

"V-sign" with his hand. He heard the kids giggling as the door was closing behind him.

"Oh, you're so cool, Richard," he said amusingly to himself.

The office was only few steps away from the front entrance. He walked in and stopped just inside the doorway. The school secretary, an elderly lady with a tall hairdo and stern look, was typing away at her desk. An assortment of succulent plants surrounded her, forming a defensive barrier of sorts.

"Excuse me," interrupted Richard.

The typing ceased and the secretary turned her head towards him. Her thin lips gave a faint smile.

"My daughter forgot to bring her lunch with her," he continued. "Can you call her classroom and let her know I've dropped it off—the name's Lizzie Reed."

"What grade?" asked the secretary.

"Grade nine."

"Grade nine?" she replied in surprise. "But Mr. Reed, the grade nines are on an all-day field trip today."

"A field trip?" he repeated, advancing a step or two.

"Yes, at the Arbor Nature Centre. You would have signed the permission form last week or she would not have been allowed to attend."

"Yes...of course," he added somewhat unsteadily, vaguely recalling having done so. "Can I take the lunch to her there?"

"Oh, I wouldn't recommend it Mr. Reed, it's at least a ninety-minute drive from here. But don't worry, they do have a small cafeteria at the Centre with sandwiches and cold drinks. I'm sure her teacher will see to it that she has lunch."

"Yes...you're right. I'm sure she'll be looked after." There was a doubtful tone in his voice.

After a slight pause he added "And what time are they expected back?"

"End of school day—3 p.m."

Richard thanked her and left the office with Lizzie's lunch bag tightly clutched in his hand.

Richard hadn't been driving for more than five minutes when he decided to turn back and head towards Oak Creek. He needed one more look at the Crimson Oak. "You're a dam fool, Richard," he murmured to himself as he drove into the parking lot. He noticed his sister's car was no longer there.

He stared at the tree for a few minutes before starting his slow walk towards it. The five branches loomed larger as he approached, their neat circular arrangement looking disturbingly unnatural. He stopped a few feet from the tree. *So,* he thought to himself, *I wasn't mistaken...* Something interfered with the symmetry between the first and fifth branches. It was the growth of a new branch...

The four schoolgirls were beginning to tire. At first, they found it easy to locate the waypoints marked on the map using their compass. The fifth and final location was, however, proving more difficult.

"I feel like we're going in circles," lamented the red-haired girl. "I'm sure we've walked by that tree several times." She pointed in the direction of a thick clump of pine trees.

"As if you could tell one tree from another, Lisa," said Grace. "You're not even wearing your glasses." There was laughter among the other girls. Then Grace added "But Lisa's right, we should have found the last location by now. Miss. Oliver said markers were only 20 minutes away from each other...maybe we are going in circles. What do you think Lizzie?"

There was no answer.

"Lizzie," she called again, turning to look behind her. The surrounding dense foliage and silence suddenly made her feel frightened. Her mouth went dry.

"Lizzie...where are you?"

Richard stopped the car at the first payphone he encountered. He dialed directory assistance and asked to be transferred to the nature centre. He glanced at his watch impatiently as he waited for the line to be answered. It was 1:30 p.m.

A young woman answered the phone "Arbor Nature Centre, how can I help you?"

"Hello, my daughter's school is visiting your centre today, I wanted to know if the kids are on their way back to school. The school's called Humberview."

"There are a lot of schools here today," she

replied. "I wouldn't know which have left. What I can tell you is that lots of kids have already started boarding the school buses. They normally start heading back at this time."

"I see," he said disappointingly. "Well, thank you anyway. Goodbye."

Troubled, he stared at the phone a few seconds before slowly hanging up the receiver. What was previously a feeling of anxiety was now turning into one of fear. *Keep it together,* he told himself as he headed for his car. He could do nothing except go to the school and wait for her bus.

Lizzie was not on the first school bus to arrive. The driver told Richard another bus was on the way, and that, no, he didn't know when it would arrive. All he knew was that there were a few kids that hadn't made their way back to the main entrance on time, so naturally the bus was delayed.

At 3:30 p.m., the second bus arrived. Richard felt weak as he waited for the doors of the bus to open. Five children exited the bus—Lizzie was not one of them. His legs gave way and he fell to his knees. His head spun, but he thought he felt a pair of arms wrap themselves around his neck and a warm cheek press against his. And just before passing out, he thought he heard the words "I'm here dad..."

Richard awoke to find himself sitting on the curb, with his back up against the side of the school bus. In front of him stood the bus driver and Lizzie's teacher, Miss. Oliver. Between them, bending forward with hands on knees, looking directly at him, was Lizzie.

Richard smiled. "First I wake up late and can't drive you to school and then I pass out when it's time to take you home. How's that for service?"

Lizzie smiled back. "Sorry I scared you dad. Guess you freaked out when I wasn't on the bus."

"That I did," he said calmly, then raised his arms for a hug.

She held his hand during the drive home. Richard glanced over at Lizzie and smiled reassuringly. Apart from her dishevelled hair, a few minor scratches and a bruised knee, she looked fine.

"I'm sorry dad," she said softly, not turning her head towards him.

"For what?"

"I lost mom's ribbon. I noticed you looked at my hair."

"Don't worry about it Lizzie. All that matters is that you're back home safely."

She gave his hand a firm squeeze then closed her eyes for the remainder of the drive.

Lizzie was in a surprisingly chatty mood over dinner, and there was plenty of laughter around the table. After the meal, Richard asked if Kimberly would mind staying with Lizzie for a while longer, as he wanted to drop by his office to check for messages.

"At this hour?" asked Kimberly.

"Best time of the day," replied Richard. "Office is empty, and I can go through the messages in peace. Besides, I'm sure there will be one or two 'urgent' ones requiring my attention first thing in the morning." He took the car keys out of his pocket and added "I shouldn't be more than an hour. I'll pick-up some ice cream on the way home. See you shortly."

As he drove, he replayed what Miss Oliver had told him about the situation. Lizzie, for reasons unknown, had separated from her group. All Lizzie remembered was tripping over a tree root, and something scratching her face as she lay on the ground. It was her best friend Grace who found her. The girl was astute enough to notice several birds dart away in alarm from a small grove of oak trees nearby. She found Lizzie there, on the ground, crying. Miss Oliver thought it best to drive Lizzie back in her car, which was why she wasn't on the bus. She was sorry but that was all the information she had...

Richard brought the car to a slow stop so that the car beams illuminated a foot path—the same one he had walked earlier that day. He had arrived at Oak Creek. Taking the two objects he had placed on the passenger seat before leaving, he started to walk down the path.

The park was pitch-black, but the lantern he brought provided enough light to guide his way. The second object was gripped tightly in his right hand. He could tell he was approaching the tree—he could sense its baneful influence, an evil that permeated the very air around it. A few more steps and it slowly came into view, casting a long shadow by the light of the lantern.

He hooked the lantern on an older branch up above and examined the new growth carefully. He was surprised to see that the newest branch had started to wither. He took a step back and, in a clear, hard voice said: "You tried to take her, but you can never have her."

The razor edge of the axe gleamed in the light as he raised it over his head, and with a vengeance he brought it down on the branch. A sharp *crack* filled the air as the metal hit its target. The severed branch fell towards the ground but came to an abrupt stop a few feet above the damp earth, as if something had reached out to stop its descent. Richard drew closer but staggered back all at once, exclaiming "Dear God in heaven ..."

Like a twisted umbilical cord, emerging from within the dangling branch and extending up into the protruding stump, was a silky, emerald-green ribbon.

A DEADLY SLICE

A Lieutenant Eastman Mystery: 1970

There are 17 payphone locations in the town of Alton, of which only two had working phones. One was at the corner of Albert Street and Mc-Dermot Avenue. The second, where Enzo found himself standing at 3 a.m. on a blustery Friday morning, was at Maryland Street, a few blocks north of the public library. Unlike the Albert Street booth, the Maryland one was on a dimly lit residential street, and Enzo had taken the extra precaution of removing the booth's overhead light.

The payphone rang at 3:02 a.m. - Enzo let it ring twice before answering with a simple "Hello."

"Do you play golf, Mr. Enzo?" inquired the calm, even voice on the other end.

"Yes," replied Enzo.

"Are you good at it?"

"Yes."

"Excellent. Then I need you to play a round of golf this morning..."

Enzo's first drive that morning was an impressive 289 yards straight down the fairway.

"Beautiful shot," said the taller of his two opponents.

"I'd say," added the other. "Selfishly, I'm relieved you're not a member of our club—you'd put many of us to shame, including me."

A faint smile broke across Enzo's face, and he gave a nod of appreciation towards his opponent.

"By the way," continued the player after a slight pause, "which club are you a member of?"

"Shadow Pine Country Club over at Stonehill county." Enzo delivered the lie with a calm, matter-of-fact voice as he walked towards the next hole.

After scoring Birdies on the first two holes,

Enzo made a costly error on the third hole—he hooked the ball severely to the left. The hole was a narrow 250 yards bordered by oak and beech trees on either side. The ball went out-of-bounds as it sailed just over a dense cluster of trees not more than 100 yards from the tee.

"Bad luck that. Do you want to declare a lost ball?" asked one of the players.

"Nope. Regulations grant me three minutes to locate the ball and that's exactly what I plan to do. You gents go ahead and take your turns. I'll meet you on the green in three minutes."

Enzo did not appear after three minutes. After waiting a few more minutes, the two men decided to go search for him.

"I'm pretty sure his ball fell in this area, but I don't see him anywhere. Where the devil could he have gone to?"

"I don't know, but isn't that his golf club up against that tree?" The other player was pointing with his club towards a large oak about twenty feet to their right. The two men approached the golf club but stopped short of picking it up. The face of the golf club was stained with a few drops of red fluid. While they looked, a new drop appeared. Both men looked up at the same time. Hanging 15 feet overhead from a branch was a strand of cloth, and it was soaked in blood.

Lieutenant Eastman parked his lime-green Ford Pinto in one of the "Reserved" parking spots near the front of the club house. A caddie, who was making his way towards the course, stopped and stared at the car in disbelief. "Porsche is in the garage," said the Lieutenant as he headed to the main doors, "had to take the family car."

He had just made his way through the sliding doors when he was approached by an aging security guard. "Excuse me sir, this is a private—" he stopped in mid-sentence, then, with a look of recognition on his face, asked "Lieutenant Eastman?"

"Lloyd Jennings, it's good to see you." The two men exchanged a warm handshake before the Lieutenant continued "But what are you doing here—I thought you retired a few years ago?"

"I retired from the force. I didn't retire from paying the bills."

Lieutenant Eastman cracked a smile. "I hear you. Both my kids are in college and there is no retirement anytime soon in my future." They spent the next few minutes reminiscing about their time together in the police force before the Lieutenant inquired about the missing golfer. "What can you tell me about the events here this morning? All I have so far is that someone went missing while playing golf and that there may be some evidence of foul play."

"I'm not able to add much more, I'm afraid." Replied Jennings. "I was doing my rounds when the front desk calls me on my radio and tells me we lost a golfer. I laugh at first, but he tells me it's no joke and to head to the front desk ASAP. There are two golfers waiting for me who confirm that the third man in their group has gone missing, and that they found his bloody golf club abandoned by a tree. I called you folks right away. A detective along with a couple of folks from Forensics arrived about 30 minutes ago. Ten minutes later, Forensics comes by again and asks if we have an aerial lift on the premises that they can use. Lucky for them we do, as we use it to update the jumbo scoreboard during tournaments—it's a good 25 feet above ground. Don't ask me why Forensics needs it. I knew better than to ask."

After a short pause, Jennings shrugged his shoulders and added "That's about all I can tell you Lieutenant. Guess you'll be wanting to get to the scene now. Follow me and I'll drive you over in one of our golf carts."

Detective Samuel Conway was looking through his notes when Lieutenant Eastman arrived on the scene. The Lieutenant quickly surveyed the area; one golf club, one rag hanging from a branch, and a pair of Forensic scientists standing in an aerial lift raised 30 feet in the air, located next to a tree.

"Good morning, Sam. What do you have so far?" Lieutenant Eastman inquired in a casual tone.

Detective Conway flipped a few pages of his notepad and stopped at the page he dog-eared earlier. He tapped the end of his pencil on the page as he skimmed the dozen or so notes he had jotted down. "According to the two golfers, Rob McKenzie and Joel Roberts, the missing person gave his name as Angelo Trifello. This was the first time they played golf with him. In fact, they had not met Mr. Trifello before today."

"How did they end-up playing together?" Inquired Lieutenant Eastman.

"Mr. Trifello was to tee off with a Mr. Rutherford—and yes, that's the wealthy owner of Rutherford and Sons Construction—at 7:00 a.m. Today's roster shows Mr. Rutherford and "guest" as the scheduled players, and apparently Mr. Trifello was the guest. Mr. Rutherford, however, was a no-show. When Mr. McKenzie and Mr. Robberts arrived for their 7:30 a.m. tee-off, Mr. Trifello asked if he could join them as the third player. They had no objection since they saw it as a great networking opportunity —that is, to connect with someone who knew Mr. Rutherford well enough to be his golfing partner."

Lieutenant Eastman nodded his head slowly then asked, "Have you checked with Mr. Rutherford?"

"I did—but his residence informed me that he was out. They expect him back by 2 p.m. I'll swing by his place before returning to the office and speak with him personally."

Detective Conway glanced down at his notes once more before continuing.

"At the third hole, Mr. Trifello hooked the ball into the area where we're standing now. Mr. McKenzie and Mr. Roberts took their turns while Mr. Trifello went to search for his ball. They were to meet on the green in a few minutes. When Mr. Trifello didn't show, they went looking for him, and that's when they noticed his golf club leaning against the tree." Detective Conway pointed with his pencil towards a large oak tree over to their right where the club was resting upright. The men walked over to the club before Detective Conway spoke again.

"The blood on the face of the club is from the rag directly above. Forensics says there's no evidence that the club was used as a weapon."

"And what about the rag?"

"Torn piece of cotton cloth. Could be from a golf polo shirt, we'll know more after we get it to the lab."

Lieutenant Eastman shifted his sight from the rag to the Forensic team directly overhead.

"Forensics has been examining the same area of this tree since I got here, which, I estimate, is a good 30 feet off the ground. What gives?"

Detective Conway flipped his notepad shut and stuck the pencil in his breast pocket before replying. "When they examined the bloody rag, they identified other droplets of blood on the branch, as well as the tree trunk. As I understand it, the shape of the droplets suggested that they fell from above, so they followed the trail up the tree to the point where the trunk forks into two main branches, which is where they are now. At that junction, the tree is partially hollowed, and..." Detective Conway hesitated for a moment, then continued "...they think they found the body at that spot."

Lieutenant Eastman dropped his head and gazed directly at the detective, then added, "Think?"

"The body can't be identified at this point. It was wedged into the tree with such intensity that it's pretty much flattened like a hamburger patty. Needless to say, they'll be there quite a while working on getting the body out."

Lieutenant Eastman slowly looked back up

at the forensic team. "What in God's name happened here…" he quietly said to himself.

Lieutenant Eastman was cutting out an article from the Alton Gazette newspaper when Detective Conway stepped just inside his office and gave a single knock on the open door.

"Come in Sam and help yourself to a cup of coffee. Brewed it less than an hour ago, so it's fresher than the stuff they're serving in the kitchen." The Lieutenant slid the article to one side as he tossed the rest of the newspaper into the wastepaper basket. "What did Mr. Rutherford have to say about his golfing partner?"

"He's never heard of an Angelo Trifello, nor did he or any of his house staff book the golfing appointment for this morning."

"I'm not surprised," replied Lieutenant Eastman. "The staff at the golf club told me they normally don't allow 7:00 a.m. tee-offs, but as it was Mr. Rutherford's name on the roster, no one questioned the booking. And no one is sure when the booking took place—could be that our mysterious Mr. Trifello added it this morning—he had opportunity. The main doors open at

7:00 a.m. but it wasn't until 7:20 a.m. that the front desk attendant started his shift."

Detective Conway nodded his head in agreement.

"How's Forensics coming along with the composite sketch?" added Lieutenant Eastman.

"All done." Detective Conway removed a sheet from the folder resting on his lap. He took a quick glance at the image before sliding it across the desk to the Lieutenant. "Both golfers agree that it is a very close likeness."

Lieutenant Eastman studied the sketch for a few moments, then added "Pretty sure I've never come across his face before. Let's get this out to our neighbouring precincts. Wouldn't hurt to send it across state lines as well. Let them know it's a person of interest—possible homicide."

"Will do." Replied Detective Conway. Then, after a slight pause, added, "Any theories?"

Lieutenant Eastman held up his notepad. The front page was blank. "And what about you?"

Detective Conway slid out a notepad from beneath his folder and held it up for the Lieutenant to see.

"Well at least your page isn't totally blank. What's that doodle in the top corner of the page?"

"Doodle?" Detective Conway turned the pad towards him. "Oh that," he added with a slight grin on his face. "That, Lieutenant, is a plane heading to Florida, or at least I think that's where it's heading. Little Jimmy is very anxious to go on vacation. He's been drawing airplanes and seashells everywhere, including on our kitchen walls."

"A plane to Florida....now that is interesting." Lieutenant Eastman placed his finger onto the newspaper clipping he had set aside and slowly slid it toward the detective.

Detective Conway picked up the clipping and raised his eyebrows as he read the headline. "Yes..." he said slowly. "Yes, I think I see what you're getting at..."

A perfect day for fishing, Amy thought to herself, as she gazed out at the placid water of Lake Pinnacle. She was disappointed that the shoreline was already crowded with joggers and sightseers at such an early hour—but what could she expect on such a beautiful weekend morning? Besides, it didn't interfere with her fishing. She knew of a secluded spot conveniently hidden by a dense grove of pine trees. Just beyond the trees, nestled peacefully within a narrow, sandy cove, there was a wooden dock that extended 15 feet out into the lake. Amy would spend a few relaxing hours fishing there while taking in the soft lake breeze and the peaceful sound of lapping waves against the pebbled shore.

As expected, there was no one about when she got there, except for a seagull floating a few feet beyond the dock. As she walked toward the end of the dock, she realized the seagull wasn't floating but perched on something dark that projected a few inches above the water. The seagull was pecking at it repeatedly, the tip of its beak turning more crimson with each additional strike. "My god," Amy said in a trembling voice, "that's the back of a person's head..." Then she screamed and screamed.

Lieutenant Eastman was on his third coffee by the time Detective Conway arrived at the precinct early Monday morning. He headed straight for the Lieutenant's office and had no sooner seated himself when the Lieutenant slid a fax across the desk towards him. "Came through about a half-hour ago from New York."

Detective Conway picked up the fax and let out a low whistle as he read its contents. "So..." he said slowly, "our missing golfer's real name is Enzo Caputo, not Angelo Trifello. Quiet a long rap sheet, including drug trafficking and money laundering. Served just over a year in state prison..." He stopped reading and glanced up at the Lieutenant before adding: "Strikes me as an awfully short sentence for such crimes."

"Yes, I noted that as well," responded the Lieutenant. "We'll need to dig into that further. In the meantime, his record suggests we're dealing with a narcotics case, so let's pull the files on some of the bigger drug players around here and see if the folks in New York can draw any connection between them and Enzo."

"Will do, Lieutenant," replied Detective Conway.

Lieutenant Eastman was about to get up and pour himself another cup of coffee when there was a knock at the door. "I'm sorry to interrupt

Lieutenant," said a junior officer standing in the doorway, "the captain assigned you a new case." He held up the manila folder he was holding in his hand. "It's a drowning that occurred at Lake Pinnacle over the weekend."

"A drowning?" inquired the Lieutenant in surprise. "We normally do not get involved with accidents."

"Oh, this was no accident, Lieutenant," responded the officer, before adding in a softer, but clear voice. "The victim was standing under water with both his feet embedded in cement blocks..."

"Good God," uttered Lieutenant Eastman gravely before extending his hand to receive the folder. He waited for the officer to leave prior to flipping the file open. He was not prepared for what he saw inside. After an appreciable interval, and without saying a word, he removed the victim photo and handed it to Detective Conway. The photo was that of Enzo Caputo.

"This," said Detective Conway grimly, "is getting very weird."

"So it appears," agreed Lieutenant Eastman,

"but it supports our belief that narcotics are at the heart of this case. Enzo must have crossed a pretty big player to end up wearing cement shoes. As for whose body is wedged in the tree trunk...I have no idea at this time."

Lieutenant Eastman leaned back in his chair and let out a long sigh, then said:

"Let's go through what we know, or can reasonably infer, so far:

"First, Enzo was at the golf course because he needed to find or accomplish something. Given his criminal record, it almost certainly had to do with narcotics. It was necessary for him to be there early, before the course became busy with other golfers.

"Second, whatever he needed to do or find, it was located off the green of the third hole. This is supported by the fact that both the golfers he played with told me he was a pro—so there's no way he would have made such a severe error on an easy hole. This leads me to believe that the slice on hole 3 was intentional—it provided the perfect cover for him to get into the area he needed to search."

Pausing to sip his cold coffee, the Lieutenant continued:

"He had only three minutes to assess the target area—not a lot of time. And by not returning to the game he must have known the other golfers would come looking for him. So why leave the game at that point?"

"Perhaps," Detective Conway added after a moment's silence, "we should take a step back and ask ourselves why send Enzo in the first place?"

"That, detective, is a very good suggestion," replied the Lieutenant, reaching for Enzo's file from the stack piled neatly beside him. "Let's have another look at his rap sheet."

The Lieutenant flipped open the file and read the case summaries out loud.

"Nothing here we didn't read before. There are some notes made by one of the investigating detectives. Let's see…seems they couldn't make a charge stick for…" The Lieutenant's voice faded as he skimmed the note with intense interest. After a brief interval, he raised his head and looked across at the detective.

"I don't know how we missed this the first

time we reviewed the file. The note states that Enzo was suspected of being a 'fixer', cleaning up evidence from crime scenes for some of the bigger drug dealers. And get this. They're pretty sure this included acting as a 'cleaner'—disposing of bodies."

"But not by stuffing them 30 feet up in a tree..." pointed out the detective. "We're not any further ahead than before."

"I disagree..." replied the lieutenant pensively as a plausible scenario took shape in his mind. "Consider the following...

"Enzo went there expecting to find *both* a body and a bag of drug money. It would take him no more than a couple of minutes to locate both. He could then rejoin the game, feign an injury after hitting his next shot as an excuse to return to the clubhouse. On his way back, he would be free to detour to the target area once again, hide the body—I suspect he would return later that evening to properly dispose of it—retrieve the money and head back to his car. No one would have been the wiser. Total time to execute would be less than 10 minutes."

"I see..." said Detective Conway thoughtfully,

"but since a body wasn't anywhere to be found, he could just take the money and leave unobserved. There was no need to return to the game. He got what he came for."

Lieutenant Eastman nodded his head in reply.

"But this doesn't explain why Enzo was killed," said the detective after a brief pause.

"Given how he was killed, there can be only one reason—he got greedy. Enzo peeks in the money bag and decides that he is looking at his retirement fund, so he makes his way back to his car and drives away with the money. He believes, mistakenly as it turns out, that he can disappear from the people he just double-crossed. By the time they realize he wasn't delivering the money, Enzo would be in Mexico with a new identity."

"All of this makes sense," Detective Conway added, "but it still leaves us in the dark as to why there was drug money at that spot to begin with, not to mention a body in a tree, and who Enzo was working for."

"Perhaps I can help you answer that last question," came a reply from the doorway. Lieutenant Eastman looked up quickly to see a clean-cut, athletic looking man wearing a blue suit. *Well, well,* the Lieutenant thought to himself, *another unexpected visitor.*

"Agent Wilson, FBI." The agent removed his identity badge from his breast pocket and held it towards the Lieutenant. "My apologies for interrupting, but I couldn't help overhearing the last part of your conversation. I was the one who sent you the fax this morning. I got on the first plane here so that I could speak with you in person."

"Apology accepted, Agent Wilson. We certainly weren't expecting the FBI to visit our small precinct, but please come in." Lieutenant Eastman motioned towards the empty chair next to Detective Conway. "This is Detective Conway, and at this point in our investigation we'd welcome any insights you could provide."

Two days later, Detective Conway found himself sitting in the passenger seat of a Ford F-150 truck. He was wearing a blue mechanic's uniform with the logo *Turbo Aviation Services* embroidered on the breast pocket. John Elliot, a qualified aviation mechanic, was driving the truck.

"How much longer?" inquired Detective Conway as he glanced down at his watch.

"We're almost there." John pointed towards the passenger side of the windshield as he answered, where a single-engine turboprop plane could be seen coming in for a landing.

Within a few minutes they were approaching the guard booth at the Genesis Flight Airfield. John greeted the security guard with a quick nod of his head before handing him his business card and adding:

"We have a meeting with a Mr. O'Brian at 10 a.m. We'll be conducting the annual inspection on his aircraft."

After confirming the appointment by ringing through to Mr. O'Brian, the guard opened the perimeter gate. "Turn right and follow the service road around the airfield—you're looking for hanger number 12 A—it's a small private hanger just beyond the main facility."

Mr. O'Brian was waiting for them by his plane—a blue and white Cessna 182 that had been modified by the removal of its passenger door. *Apollo Skydiving* was written in red letters across the fuselage.

The men introduced themselves, with Detective Conway using the name "Frank Doyle" as his alias. After a few preliminary questions about the plane's condition, Mr. O'Brian was handed a few forms to initial. At this point, Detective Conway said "The inspection will take about an hour. I did want to let you know that we offer a 15% discount on cash payments—you'll pay just $175. Parts, if required, are of course extra."

Mr. O'Brian handed the initialed forms back to Detective Conway, then added in a casual tone "Sounds fair. Cash it is."

Lieutenant Eastman and Agent Wilson were seated on a park bench located across from the police station, awaiting Detective Conway's return. At 11:45 a.m., a Ford F-150 truck drove up to the curb and out stepped Detective Conway from the passenger side.

"Why, if it isn't aviation mechanic Frank Doyle," said Lieutenant Eastman with a smile. "So, tell us, did the client take the discount?"

Detective Conway reached into his back pocket and pulled out a white sealed envelope.

"Excellent work detective," said Agent Wilson as he took the envelope. "I'll have my team check the numbers. It shouldn't take long to know if we have a match."

Within an hour of receiving a positive confirmation from Agent Wilson, Mr. O'Brian was arrested on charges of trafficking narcotics and money laundering.

That evening, the three men had returned to Lieutenant Eastman's office to discuss the case.

"So," began Agent Wilson, "do you folks feel like you have enough evidence to build a convincing case against O'Brian?"

"I believe we do, in large part thanks to you," said the Lieutenant. "There are some assumptions we'll need to make in order to tie everything together, especially when it comes to the events that transpired at the golf course."

"I still have an hour before my plane leaves for New York. I'm all ears, if you're up to reviewing the case with me."

"I'll take you up on that," answered the Lieutenant. "Let's begin with the two pieces of critical information that you provided to us. First,

Enzo was an FBI informant, which explained the short prison term mentioned in the fax you sent over—a reduced sentence in exchange for becoming an informant. Secondly, O'Brian hired Enzo for select 'jobs', primarily those involving local payment pickups from the sale of narcotics. It wasn't long before Enzo informed you that he believed O'Brian was using his plane to transport narcotics across state lines. The plane would depart late in the evening carrying narcotics and return in the early hours of the morning with cash from the sale of the drugs."

"That's correct," concurred Agent Wilson.

"Knowing this," continued the Lieutenant, "you gave Enzo the name of an interested buyer in Florida that he was to pass on to O'Brian. What neither man knew was that the buyer was an FBI agent. After stalling for months, O'Brian finally decided to go ahead with the deal, the sale of a quarter of a million dollar's worth of narcotics. His plane arrived in Florida last Friday at 12:30 a.m., and the exchange was made. Of course, O'Brian would not be present at these deals, but if you could link him directly to spending or depositing the drug money, then it would provide supporting evidence to Enzo's previous testimonies that O'Brian was behind the drug deals. In order to accomplish this, the serial numbers of the bills used to purchase the drugs were recorded by your team prior to the exchange."

Agent Wilson nodded his head in agreement.

The Lieutenant paused for a moment to arrange his thoughts, then said:

"So, how do we tie this to the events that occurred at the golf course? How did the drug money get there, why was a body found wedged in a tree, and why was Enzo killed?

"Let's begin with explaining Enzo's death," continued Lieutenant Eastman. "After receiving your fax, we knew we were dealing with a narcotics case. We reasoned that Enzo was at the golf course to retrieve drug money and dispose of a body that was supposed to be nearby, but unknown to anyone at the time, the body was wedged in the trunk of a tree some 30 feet above the ground. Without a body to dispose of, Enzo used the opportunity to take the money in the belief that he had enough time to vanish and enjoy a luxurious retirement. Unfortunately for him, his car was probably under surveillance from O'Brian's men, given how much money was as stake. Once Enzo drove away, it wouldn't have taken them long to realize he wasn't planning on delivering the money. As a result, they gave him cement boots as a retirement gift."

"And what about the body in the tree?" asked Agent Wilson, "How did it get there?"

"The only possible way it could get there," answered Lieutenant Eastman. "The body fell from the sky. That afternoon I came across a newspaper article that caught my attention—I have it here." The Lieutenant pulled out the clipping from his desk and read:

"*Mystery Plane Heard Flying Over Golf Course During Dead of Night. Residents living near the Alton Golf and Country Club are upset over a plane that flies-by during the early hours of the morning. The plane has been heard several times this year...*"

The Lieutenant passed the newspaper clipping to Agent Wilson before continuing.

"In order to avoid detection, a plane like O'Brian's would need to fly fairly low, the typical *modus operandi* in the illegal narcotics trade. The pilot would navigate by dead reckoning, using visual ground references, like the *Alton Golf and Country Club*, to navigate to and from the airfield. I suspect that as the plane was flying over the golf course, the passenger fell out of the plane along with the bag full of money—as simple as that. The bag hit the ground, while the victim encountered a tree while falling at a speed of 100 mph. We know the weather bureau issued a wind advisory for early that Friday morning, especially dangerous weather for low flying planes. Sudden turbulence could have caused the plane to bank violently as it flew over the golf course. As O'Brian's skydiving plane has no passenger door, both the victim and the money were ejected from the plane. Despite the danger, the plane probably continued to circle the area until it spotted the location of the bag. I can't imagine the pilot returning to the airfield unless he could tell O'Brian *exactly* where his money landed. Enzo was then hired to retrieve the money and dispose of the body believed to be on the ground."

"Makes sense," agreed Agent Wilson, "and it shouldn't be too difficult to trace the pilot to corroborate your theory. O'Brian's trusted circle of 'employees' is small. We'll send you the names of possible suspects to question by tomorrow."

"And finally," said Lieutenant Eastman, "we have Detective Conway, or should I say 'Frank Doyle', to thank for the arrest of O'Brian. By offering a cash discount for the plane inspection, O'Brian paid with the recorded bills, as you suspected he would."

"Once again detective," said Agent Wilson "let me congratulate you on a job well done."

The men discussed one or two other minor points of the case before Agent Wilson arose from his seat and said: "Well, I best be off to catch my plane. I'm sure we'll be speaking with each other over the next couple of weeks as you finalize the case against O'Brian. Good luck gentlemen and thank you for your cooperation."

As the agent's footsteps died away, Lieutenant Eastman said: "Well Sam, this case has certainly been one for the books. Could it have been any stranger?"

"Not unless we encounter Enzo walking around in cement shoes..."

Lieutenant Eastman chuckled, then said pleasantly "C'mon Sam, I'll buy you dinner at Fran's. Please switch off the lights on the way out."

"Will do Lieutenant, will do…"

A native of Ontario, Canada, Stephen intertwines his academic prowess with a lifelong passion for the paranormal. With a Master of Science and Business, his career has spanned writing scientific and business papers, but it's his discovery of Algernon Blackwood's "The Willows" twenty years ago that ignited his love for dark and weird fiction. Growing up with tales of "true" ghost stories from his grandparents' séances and after-school sessions with "The Twilight Zone" and "Alfred Hitchcock Presents", Stephen has cultivated a deep-seated fascination for stories that delve into the horror and paranormal genres. Stephen brings a unique blend of scholarly insight and personal intrigue to his writing, creating tales that not only entertain but also resonate with a chilling touch of authenticity. *The Inheritance and Other Dark Tales* is his second book.

9 781777 282737